Return to Xa

John McKenna moved from his native Scotland nearly twenty years ago, to be near his family in South Devon. He had a long career as a Paramedic in the Royal Navy and in Health and Social Care and the Voluntary Sector. He is now happily retired - but not from life!

When he's not writing - John loves walking Devon's coastal paths and nearby Dartmoor and spending time with his family. He has written poetry and short stories since childhood. His short story: Hotel Capo De Bonta, is published - in the South Hams Authors Network Anthology of short stories, 'Grasping the Nettle.'

Return to Xanthos is his debut novel.

RETURN TO
Xanthos

by

John McKenna

Copyright ©2024 John McKenna
All rights reserved.

The right of John McKenna to be identified as the Author of the Work has been asserted by him in accordance with the Copyright Designs and Patents Act 1988.

All rights reserved. No part of this publication may be reproduced, stored in a retrieval system or transmitted in any form or by any means without the prior consent of the author, nor be otherwise circulated in any form of binding or cover other than that in which it is published without a similar condition, being imposed on the subsequent publisher.

ISBN: 9798879685176

Disclaimers

This is a work of fiction. Historical events are either factually real or inspired by real life events, but the characters and their interactions are entirely imaginary.

Acknowledgements

I am indebted to writer friends from the Ivybridge Library Writers Group and the South Hams Authors Network and in particular Tony Rea and Figgy Mack. Thanks also to my son-in-law Kelvin James, for the huge amount of work he did formatting my novel and cover design.

Dedication

Dedicated to the beloved memory of Teresa (Tess) McKenna.

1
THE PARTY

Grant and Jude's house was down a winding track - on a hill just outside the town of Neo Chorio. Their garden had fantastic views of the Aegean Sea on one side and an olive clad valley, dotted with tall thin cypress trees on the other. The cicadas were still chirping their Mediterranean chorus as the guests arrived. Smells of delicious food wafted over the garden and the murmur of conversation and music and laughter echoed around their isolated house. They were fantastic hosts and had prepared amazing food, myriads of Greek dishes, kleftiko, aubergines in olive oil, dolmades, fat glossy black Kalamata olives, feta and tomato salad, fresh baked bread and lots of other mezes. They were old hands at this and drinks were dispensed in large measures. It wasn't long before the garden was buzzing with laughter and warm conversation.

Jude pointed to the spot near where they'd set up a makeshift bar...'We're thinking of building a holiday cottage over there beside our studios - extra cash always comes in handy. Our pensions don't go far these days.'

Simon ambled over to a small knot of people surrounding Jude.

'Welcome Simon darling.' Jude kissed him on both cheeks.

'Hi Jude, what about you - thanks for inviting me.'

'We're fine, thanks darling and It's our pleasure. Grant told me that you're going to be finishing that house of yours - it needs to be lived in.'

'You're right Jude - as always.'

'Oh look, here's Mags. How's you darling?' she said as she reached out to kiss her friend.

'How are ya Jude?' Mags drew on her customary fat roll up.

Maggie *Mags* Morrison stood around five feet three, she was reed slim, with cropped grey hair that suited her elfin features. Her skin was mahogany from years in the sun, and her fingers were festooned with gold rings, her signature look, as a famous young Scottish rock chick in the seventies.

'How's it going Mags, haven't seen you for a while?' Simon enquired.

She inhaled deeply on her cigarette. 'Oh you know, just livin my life, drinkin my whisky and gettin by.'

'Still singing?'

'Yeah now and then, for the tourists you know?' she said, languidly.

'Grand - here's to you.' Simon took a slug of his Metaxa and coke.

His best friend and partner in crime, Panos, his wife Eleni and some others were gathered at the bottom of the garden.

'He's still drinking a lot,' Panos observed.

'Grief affects people in different ways. They were a close couple - it must be hard for him,' Eleni replied.

'We'll keep an eye on him, don't worry,' Grant said. He seemed distracted and looked over to the far side of the garden and frowned. 'Sorry, must go folks, that bloody bore Ruthven's arrived, I can't stand him, best be polite though, as I'm the host.'

Grant shook hands with Major (Ret'd) Donald Ruthven.

'Evening Donald, Jenny, how are we?' Grant enquired, looking up at his six feet four guest.

'Well,' he boomed, 'apart from the fact that you've already run out of my bloody favourite Scotch, I suppose I'll survive.'

Simon watched the little scene unfold from a distance. *Arsehole*, he thought.

He walked past Ruthven and his wife - on his way to the bar.

'Hey McCardle, are you still here? I thought you'd given up on us and decided to return to the bogs!'

Simon shook his head. 'Evening Donald, Mrs Ruthven,' Simon replied, with admirable restraint.

'Ignore him, silly old fool,' Jude said, walking beside him.

Simon shook his head. 'You'd think I'd been in the Provisional fucking IRA, the way he goes on - I left Belfast when I was eighteen.'

Jude sighed. 'I know. I only invited him because Jenny's my friend. He's such a bully though. That woman should be made a saint.'

'Doesn't he know Siobhan died?'

'Yes of course he does. I told Jenny not long after it happened,' she replied. Get yourself another drink and come and talk to Naomi and her husband, they've not long moved here.'

'Ok Jude, whatever you say.'

Jude led him over to the young couple. They had a brief chat - but he wasn't really listening.

'Just going to speak to the Major, Jude,' Simon said abruptly.

'Darling please don't - you know how you two wind each other up. Don't spoil your good news.' She pulled at his arm. He shook it off.

'I'm fine Jude, let me be. I just want a word.'

He walked over slightly unsteadily to join Ruthven's group. 'Evening Donald, Mrs Ruthven.'

'Well...if it isn't Paddy McCardle. Where have you been hiding?'

Simon raised his voice 'My name's Simon...as you're very well aware... and I haven't been hiding anywhere...My wife died - didn't you hear!'

'I may have done - can't remember,' the Major replied, dismissively - and drank a large measure of his scotch.

'Donald, I told you months ago - that poor Siobhan had died,' Jenny, his wife said.

Most people had stopped chatting and were looking around to see what the commotion was.

Ruthven's face was becoming redder by the minute. 'I can't be expected to remember everything that happens around here. His wife was a pain in the arse anyway- a bloody hippy - full of herself.'

'Don - that is enough now, you are totally out of order,' Jenny said.

Simon moved forward quickly and punched him on the mouth. Ruthven stumbled backwards and fell over the barbeque and landed on the grass, followed by a table and bottles and glasses.

Simon stood over him. 'If you *ever* talk that way about my wife again...I'll fuckin kill you! Is that understood!'

Silence.

He kicked Ruthven hard in the balls and he screamed in pain.

'I said - is that understood - you bigoted bastard!'

'Yes, yes,' Ruthven whimpered, curling up in a ball.

'Simon, Stop!' Panos shouted.

He and Grant grabbed Simon and held him back. He still looked fighting mad.

***

The next day Panos and Simon sat outside Panos's taverna.

'You caught him a good one. He squealed like a pig?' Panos said.

'Serves the bastard right. I've been wanting to do that for fucking ages.' He winced as he felt his right hand, it was puffy and red.

'Yes, he has been asking for it for many years. I nearly punched him myself for what he said about Siobhan.'

'Like a few more I bet. I don't suppose we'll be seeing his ugly mug at parties for a while though. I'll bet he'll press charges,' Simon said.

'We'll see,' said Panos. I hope not. Put it out of your mind for now and let's talk about happier things - like this house you're supposed to be finishing. That's why you came back here, my friend.'

'I know. I need to get to work, get my hands dirty.'

'I'll talk to Georgios, he will show you the ropes,' Panos replied.

Eleni was in the kitchen, preparing for the day ahead. She waved over at Simon and he raised his hand and smiled. Panos was lucky, he thought, a beautiful wife, lovely kids, a thriving business and an idyllic place to live. He envied him. The sound of children's laughter brought him out of his thoughts. He spotted Dimitri. 'Hello Dimitri, how are you my friend?'

'Fine Mr Simon,' he said shyly. He was sixteen years old and the double of his father.

'Come on hurry up, we'll be late for school.' He addressed his younger sister Roula.

'I'm coming. You are so impatient just like Papa.'

Simon smiled to himself. If Dimitri was like his father, ten year old Roula was the spitting image of Eleni, same raven hair, and big soulful brown eyes. Both of them waved at Simon as Eleni ushered them on the path to school. 'Children eh.' She looked up to the heavens and then at Simon. 'Sorry Simon, not very sensitive of me.'

'No it's fine, I'd have liked to have children…but we just never got around to it - too wrapped up in each other.'

Eleni put her hand gently on his shoulder and walked back into the kitchen.

***

It was late October and the house was coming on. Simon had turned up every day to help with the work, mixing concrete and plaster, his writer's soft hands became scratched and bleeding with the unaccustomed work. Soon the walls were finished and the windows were in. There was a big lounge, with a huge window that provided amazing views out over the harbour far below, a small kitchen, one big master bedroom with a balcony that gave even better views, and two smaller bedrooms which looked out onto an olive grove, and two bathrooms. It was built in the traditional island style, and had been sympathetically designed, to fit in with the neighbouring houses. It would need painting, and the roof needed to be put on quickly before the storms arrived. The garden surrounding the house was around half an acre and was stuffed full of hundreds of olive trees, many of them gnarled, ancient and pock marked, like old men's faces. Their silver blue leaves danced in the strong sunlight. There wasn't time to harvest Simon's olives this year. That would have to wait for next year and be the responsibility of whoever bought the house. At the bottom of the garden stood an old and rusted olive press. Simon wanted to keep it, and maybe clean it up and paint it. In the adjacent fields all the olives had been harvested and the last of the tourists had left before *Okhi Day*,the Greek Day of Independence on the 28th October. It was tradition that fires were lit and parties held in the tavernas and people's houses and the season's profits counted. The swallows had flown back north again.

Simon was relaxing at home one Friday afternoon, when he heard a knock at the door and when he opened it, two policemen stood before him. He recognised one of them as a nephew of Panos.

'Simon McCardle?' the taller one asked.

'Yes.'

'We are here following a complaint received from a Mr Donald Ruthven. May we come in sir?'

'Yes of course - please follow me.'

'Mr Ruthven has alleged that on the evening of Saturday 16th October, you assaulted him, at the home of Mr Grant and Mrs Jude Meakin.'

'What do you have to say sir?'

'It's true, he insulted Siobhan, my wife...my late wife...she died eight months ago. Ruthven said horrible things about her. I was very angry and upset. I shouldn't have assaulted him, I know that now, but he'd also made a racist remark to me, just before he said those horrible things about my late wife.'

'We are aware of the provocation. That does not mean you can go around punching and kicking elderly gentlemen Mr McCardle, even if they *are* being obnoxious.'

'I know.'

We need to take a statement from you and then interview more witnesses. I have to inform you that if you are found guilty, you could face a large fine or even time in prison.'

'Understood,' Simon replied.

The policemen spent the next hour taking Simon's statement and checking and re-checking it. He saw them to the front door and they drove away.

***

Simon slapped cement against the big trowel. He'd become quite expert at this work over the past few months. 'We'll soon have this wall finished, Georgios.'

Panos's cousin gave a big belly laugh. 'You are becoming quite good at this my friend,' he said admiringly.'Maybe next year a swimming pool, hah.'

'We've just the roof to finish and it's almost ready to go on the market for next season,'

'It is a good house and will sell to people wanting to retire here - or a holiday home. Where will *you* live?'

Simon pondered. 'Don't know, maybe stay on at the taverna, if Panos will have me. I may go back to London. I really don't know. There's so many memories here.'

'Of course, but why not live here over the winter at least, it will keep the house warm and dry. It is better for the new timbers and plaster, and the rains will be here soon,' Georgios added, looking up at the sky.

Simon considered the suggestion. 'Yeah I think I might do that, if we get it finished in time that is. I'll get out from under Panos' feet too.'

Georgios inhaled on his cigarette. 'You are a good friend to him and he is to you. We will finish it, don't worry. Things will work out my friend,' he added reassuringly.

***

The weather suddenly changed a few days later. Thunderstorms filled the skies and rain lashed down for days, accompanied by driving winds. The building work was put on hold for a few days. Most tourists would never see this and would no doubt be horrified that their idyll of a Greek Island was now cold and damp. The locals occupied themselves after a long hard season, by hunting in the hills, and cooking hearty Stifado stews and gossiped and caught up with friends and families, who they'd seen so little of during the season. Some shut up their houses and went on holidays themselves, or to families abroad, to rejuvenate and to enjoy their hard earned profits.

2
UNEXPECTED FERRY

Simon had settled into a routine and occupied most of his mornings in his room above the taverna, writing an article for a new island tourist magazine. He was in the habit of regularly walking into town - to sit outside Pappas restaurant and read his newspaper, as he still wanted to know what was going on in the world - ever the old journalist. As he sipped on his latte, he noted the headlines and the date - as all former journalists did: 22nd November 2017. It reported the trial in the International Criminal Tribunal for the former Yugoslavia - of Ratko Mladic - the former Serbian General. He had just been given several life sentences for war crimes, after years awaiting trial. *Serves the murdering old bastard right - Karma*, Simon thought.

***

December seemed to drag by in a haze. Simon had foregone his usual Christmas Day invitation from Panos and Elenis and the numerous New Year parties celebrating the forthcoming year of 2018. He didn't feel up to partying and mixing with people right now and had become a bit of a hermit and had hunkered down in his new home. Thankfully Georgios and his men had managed to put the roof on and make it watertight. The house smelt of plaster and brick dust and fresh paint, but he'd furnished it in a basic way and made it a bit homely. He lit his big open fire every day now. The winds howled outside most of the time, although there were occasional bright days. He was back into the routine of writing again and he could feel his creative energy slowly returning.

***

One evening in early January he heard a persistent knock at the door. The wind was blowing heavily and rain lashed against the new window panes. *Who the hell could that be in this weather?* Simon thought. He pulled open the heavy oak door and the rain and wind blew in, pushing him backwards into the hallway.

'Come in, you're soaked.'

Panos rushed into the hallway, the wind blowing in behind him, dripping water onto the marble floor. 'My God, it's crazy out there and I've not walked that far from the car, what a storm.'

Simon shut the door, only by leaning against it with his full body weight. He hung Panos's wet jacket and hat by the fire and and he began heating some water for coffee.

'What brings you here in this - you mad bugger?' Simon asked.

'The big overnight ferry from Crete to Athens is in trouble. It lost power due to the storm and high seas. My cousin said that the tugs are trying to get a rope aboard and tow it in. This happens now and then as you know.'

'Yes I remember - last time was a few years ago. Do you think they'll be ok?'

Panos sighed, 'I hope so, if the storm dies down a bit then they can bring it in under tow and berth it in the harbour.'

'Here mate.' He handed Panos a steaming cup of black Greek coffee and raised his own cup to his lips. 'Let's hope they're safe.'

'Let us pray,' said Panos looking upwards, 'Let us pray.'

The next morning the storm hadn't calmed down much and the sea was still rough. The sun was trying vainly to break through some malevolent black clouds. Panos had phoned and updated Simon on the latest news. The big beast of a ferry had been brought alongside. It was a hazardous operation, but the Greek maritime rescue service were very experienced in these types of rescues.

'They think the storm will last another few days at least. The ferry has some damage and needs to be repaired. All the passengers have gone into town,' Panos explained.

'Are you gonna open up then?'

'It's not worth the trouble my friend, but a couple of restaurants and hotels in town have opened to look after them, so they'll cash in no doubt. There are about five hundred of them and most are staying at the Port Hotel. It's strange to see the town so full of people at this time of year. Anyway I have a few things to do, I'll see you later.'

'Ok, speak to you later mate.'

Simon walked to the big lounge window and picked up his binoculars from the table. He saw that the big Athens ferry was listed to one side, leaning against the harbour wall - like a drunken giant. He peered through the misty gloom and he could just make out its name. *Minos Lines Piraeus, Pride of the Aegean*.

'Poor buggers - stranded here,' he said out loud. Still, there were worse places to spend a few days and the ferry company would pick up the tab for their stay. He showered and had a light breakfast before putting on some warm clothing and a heavy jacket and started walking through the lanes onto the main road that descended steeply into town. It was brighter now, but still raining lightly. He watched the wind bend the olive and cypress trees as he walked down towards town. It made the same eerie howling sound that had kept him awake, but the air was clean and fresh.

It took around half an hour to reach the harbour and he spotted the behemoth of a vessel right away. Its huge hull rose up hundreds of feet above the jetty and the ropes used to tie it to bollards were thicker than his arm. There was lots of activity. A knot of officials and crew members jostled about the bottom of the gangway and a large yellow crane was parked by the bows. He could make out a long gash in the starboard side of the ship, where Panos said it had collided with the harbour wall, whilst being brought alongside.

'Kalimera.'

Panos' familiar voice boomed out over the bustle and Simon walked over to him.

'Some size huh,' he said looking upwards.

'Yeah what a beast eh,' Simon replied.

They stood gazing up at it for a while, and Panos gossiped with the dock workers, as he knew them all. Then they walked over to a coffee shop by the jetty. It was hot inside and packed with rescued passengers and noisy with their conversation and the clinking of crockery. The owner Yianni was doing a brisk trade. Panos waved over at him in acknowledgment and they found the only empty table.

'My cousin says that the repair will take some weeks,' Panos said in a conspiratorial tone, as he sipped his coffee. He loved the intrigue and gossip of it all. His cousin worked in the docks and was privy to all the goings on around the harbour.

'You're such an old woman,' Simon teased.

'Well I need to know what's going on in my own town.'

'Of course you must, you nosey bugger.'

Panos nudged Simon.

'What is it?'

'Over there,' he whispered, motioning over his shoulder.

'What?'

'Can't you see?' he whispered.

Simon craned his neck and saw the object of Panos's attention. She was wearing a blue heavy duty waterproof jacket, and was seated at a table on her own reading a book. He guessed she was in her mid to late forties, with dark hair and an olive complexion.

'What a beauty eh?' Panos drooled.

'For God's sake control yourself - you're a married man.'

'Yes but a man can look.' He pointed to his right eye and pulled the eyelid down in the familiar Greek gesture.

'Yeah well she's alright I suppose,' Simon said

'Alright? Have you taken a good look?'

'Not interested mate. It's not even been a year since Siobhan died.'

'I know,' Panos replied softly.

Simon drained the last of his coffee. 'Come on let's go for a walk, it's too crowded in here.'

As they approached the door, he saw Panos take a long lascivious look at the stranger. She looked up from her book and met his gaze, then looked over at Simon and shook her head, then she returned to her book. She had huge brown eyes, but they weren't welcoming. She glared at both of them, as Simon attempted a weak silent gesture of apology for his friend's behaviour. As they exited the café, Panos was still in his reverie. 'My God did you ever see such a gorgeous woman.'

Simon pulled his friend's jacket and led him down the street.'You - my friend need a cold shower. How about I throw you in the harbour to cool off?'

***

Later that evening Simon sat at his laptop. He'd nearly finished the article describing island life and how it had changed over the years, and was pleased with it. He found himself thinking of the woman in the cafe. Panos was right, she was lovely. He thought. *I'm not dead yet, I can still appreciate an attractive woman.*

The next morning at around 10am he heard a knock at the door. It was the two policemen who had visited him a few weeks previously.

'May we come in, Mr McCardle,' the older one asked.

'Of course.' Simon replied.

The policeman took out his notebook and flipped the pages. 'You will recall that we visited you several weeks ago, concerning the alleged assault on Mr Donald Ruthven.'

'Yes of course.'

We're here to inform you that the charges against you have been dropped. I believe that Mr Ruthven's wife persuaded her husband. You can consider yourself very fortunate Mr McCardle.'

'Well, I can't say that I'm not relieved. It's been hanging over me.'

'We're aware of that sir, however, we would advise you to please keep your temper in check - if this ever happens again - which we hope it does not. There are better ways of dealing with these things, no matter how severe the provocation.'

'I know - thank you.'

'Thank you for your time sir. Have a pleasant day.'

***

Three weeks later he sat by the window in his lounge sipping a coffee and looking out to sea with his binoculars. Panos had texted him earlier that morning with the news that the ferry had been repaired and was leaving - to resume its journey to Athens. He could just make out the stern slowly disappearing from view. He placed his binoculars back on the window sill, then he went outside for some fresh air. The wind had dropped and blue skies had returned. When he came back inside his mobile was ringing.

'The ferry has gone.' It was Panos - straight to the point as always.

'I know, I've just watched it mate,' Simon replied. 'I'll bet Yianni's counting his unexpected profits.'

'Yes...and the lovely lady will be gone too,' added Panos.

3
A GREEK EASTER

The late March skies finally brought better weather. Simon was a guest at Panos's daughter Roula's birthday celebrations. The talk was of the coming season and how much money could be made in these difficult times. Eleni sidled up to him and stroked his shoulder affectionately. 'How are you?'

He looked at her and felt the warmth of friendship and caught the scent of her perfume. It had been a while since he'd been so close to a woman. He felt an urge inside him, once so familiar and an irrational sense of guilt about it for some reason, as if this was somehow being unfaithful. 'Not bad, not bad. You know Eleni, you look more beautiful every day. I envy you two, how long has it been now?'

She blushed. 'Twenty five years, we were married very young…we have our moments, as you know. So…what plans do you have for the season?'

'Well, maybe do some more writing - then I suppose I need to find a buyer for the house.'

'You still want to sell?'

'I think so, I'll see what happens. I need the money, apart from anything else.'

'Of course. Money is important.'

Eleni nodded and smiled. 'Oh I nearly forgot. Panos said to tell you he saw that woman on the other side of the island, near Agia Ekaterina, when he was fishing with his cousin, he saw her on the beach.'

'What woman?' He tried to sound casual.

'You think I don't know when a stranger is around the island - remember this is Xanthos not Crete?

Simon smiled. 'Oh I think I know who you mean. I thought she'd gone back with the ferry?'

'Apparently not.' Eleni raised her eyebrows, as she went off to fill his glass.

He thought about what Eleni had said. It could have been anyone Panos had seen, he knew what he was like, making up stories and having a good laugh at his expense.

***

Several days later, he was doing some shopping in town, when he spotted the mystery woman. She was wearing a pair of faded blue jeans, a pink t-shirt, and a thick cream coloured jumper. She was picking some tomatoes outside a mini - supermarket. He was almost alongside her, when she turned around to enter the shop and nearly bumped into him.

'Oops sorry!' she said.

'Sorry,' he replied, sounding a bit flustered.

He noticed that she had a strong accent but it wasn't Greek.

She looked at him quizzically. 'You're the man from the dockside cafe back in January - you have a good memory - your little friend is not with you today?'

'No. Look I'm sorry about that, Panos is well...you know.'

'Yes, a typical Greek male perhaps, thinks he is Adonis himself.'

Simon smiled. 'I guess so. We've been friends for years. I'm used to him - I suppose it just washes over me.'

'It is ok - I can look after myself.'

'So...planning to stay awhile?'

She ignored his question.

'Forgive me, but where are you from?

'More questions - Bosnia and Herzegovina if you must know.'

'Ah, I was trying to guess. It was so sad what happened to your country. I see that monster Mladic has finally been sentenced. It must have been difficult to have that all brought up again, after so long.'

'Yes, it wasn't easy,' she said, and then quite abruptly. 'Well, I must finish my shopping.'

'Of course, nice seeing you again.'

'Goodbye.'

He watched her walk away down a side street and thought. *'God what a bloody eejit you made of yourself there mate, Get a grip man. Your wife's not long gone and you're behaving like a schoolboy.'*

***

It was lunchtime and Simon was in his garden with Panos. The sun cast shadows on his newly laid lawn, surrounded by a forest of olive trees.

'So you saw her, talked to her. You should get to know her, ask her for a drink,' Panos said, grinning mischievously.

'Bugger off. I was embarrassed, and I had to apologise for *You*, you horny old goat.'

Panos laughed, then drained the rest of his beer. 'Seriously man, ask her out. Siobhan would be wanting you to get on with your life.'

Panos sat back in his chair. 'You know... Papou used to say, there is a land of the living and a land of the departed...and never should they meet. You must live your life.'

Simon nodded. 'Your grandad was a wise man.'

***

Soon the early April sun grew stronger, after months of changeable weather, flowers blossomed and the sound of cicadas filled the afternoon air. The first tourists landed, mainly Brits, Germans and Scandinavian, their pale skin, gradually darkening as the days went by. The town soon filled up with them and shopkeepers finished putting on the last lick of paint, and got up early to hose the dust from their shops and restaurant fronts in preparation for the coming season. Simon had joined Panos and his family for the traditional Greek Easter church service on Holy Saturday. They stood in the little church above the town with the rest of the congregation, the flickering of dozens of candle flames lit the ancient spectacle. The same scenes were being repeated all over Greece at this moment.

The black clad priests intoned their prayers solemnly, as a mock up of the tomb of Christ, along with his icon, decorated with hundreds of flowers, was carried by the priests out of the church and along the dusty path to the graveyard. The congregation silently followed, old and young alike, holding candles, lit in memory of the dead. In all his years visiting the island Simon had never witnessed this. He thought about the traditions of his own faith back in Ireland and was transported back to childhood and the service of Benediction. He remembered being a ten year old altar boy and the pungent and exotic smell of the incense - as it rose from the thurible burner he held in his hands, swinging it back and forth in unison to the priest's prayers.

The procession slowed as they reached the little graveyard and the priest said some more prayers for the deceased. Panos glanced over in the semi-darkness at the graves of his parents. Eleni took his hand and smiled gently. Her parents were buried there too. Both sets of parents had always attended these services over the years. They were strict Greek Orthodox church goers and took their faith seriously, as did most of their generation. The priest started the short journey back to the church. The air was still and the stars were out, giving the service an even more magical atmosphere. When the priest and the congregation were back inside the church, Papa Kyriakos, the parish priest, respectfully and tenderly kissed the image of Christ and just before midnight all the lights in the church were extinguished, to imitate the silent tomb of the dead Christ. Then, after a period of silence, the priest lit his candle first and passed the light to his neighbour, who did likewise, and so it carried on. Everyone passed the light to their neighbour, until the little church was bathed in an ethereal illumination. The smells of the burning candles suffused into the air. 'Christos Anesti.' *Christ has risen*, the priests intoned solemnly. 'Alithos Anesti.' *He has risen indeed*,' came the response from the assembled congregation. There was an air of celebration as they walked into the little lane outside the church, as the bells rang out into the still night air breaking the silence, and people talked excitedly to family and friends. Simon followed them and watched in awe as the twinkling lights of dozens of candles punctuated the inky blackness, as people celebrated the rising of Christ from the tomb.

Back at Panos and Eleni's house, Eleni heated the traditional *Magiritsa* soup, made from lambs' offal and flavoured with lemon, which she'd prepared days before. It was surprisingly delicious and this was followed by cloyingly sweet tasting pastries and cakes.

Simon finished his pastry and dabbed his mouth with a paper napkin. 'That was amazing. In all the time I've been here, I've never been to the Easter service. Thanks so much for inviting me. It was very moving. Now, I'd better catch up on my beauty sleep before tomorrow. I'm really looking forward to it.'

'You are very welcome,' Eleni replied.

'Kalinichta everyone. See you tomorrow.'

'Kalinichta Simon,' all the family chorused. Panos saw him out the door and shook hands, as he got in his car and drove off into the night.

***

The next morning Easter Sunday arrived with azure blue skies and a warm Spring breeze. The flowers were out in profusion and their scent filled the air. Panos had got out of bed very early, to prepare the lamb for roasting on the spit. He was assisted by his son Dimitri and together they smeared the lamb in olive oil, lemon juice, sage and wild garlic. Sprigs of rosemary were pushed into the carcass. They had previously dug a pit and set up the roasting spit. It had been handed down through the family for generations and was black with smoke from decades of use. If it could talk it would tell many tales. The exact depth of the pit was very important and they took care and pride over its preparation. Once they were satisfied, they shovelled huge amounts of charcoal and logs into the deep pit and set fire to it, with a healthy dose of petrol to help it on its way. Panos lit the fire.

'Wow,' Dimitri exclaimed, falling comically backwards onto the grass verge, as the petrol caught fire with a whooshing sound.

'Stay back,' Panos warned, laughing. You'll lose those pretty eyebrows that Mama loves on her little boy.'

Dimitri reddened with embarrassment, then picked up a stick of olive wood and gently poked it into his father's ribs.

'Ahhh!' Panos shouted in mock pain. 'Steady boy, your old man can still pack a punch.'

Then he pulled Dimitri to him in his blackened hands. Dimitri squirmed away, smiling. Roula came running towards her father and gave him a huge hug, before striding quickly away to re-join her mother.

Eleni and Roula busied themselves in the traditional Easter Sunday preparations. They began setting up tables and chairs in the big garden opposite the taverna and placing white linen tablecloths and plates and knives and forks and spoons on to long tables, set out under the shelter of the trees.

Panos shouted over. 'Ella Dimtri! Come and help me roll the wine barrels out. Your old papa needs your young muscles.'

'Of course Papa. How much have you made this year?'

'Three huge barrels and it's like nectar from the gods of Mount Olympus,' he added proudly. Panos beckoned Dmitri with a silent gesture of his hand. They both walked over to a small store at the bottom of the garden. Eleni and Roula were still busy in the garden. Panos unlocked the door to the shed with great ceremony and flicked on the light switch. Then he slowly shut the door behind him.

'Come here,' he whispered. He put his finger to his mouth to signify silence.

'What is it Papa?' Dimitri lowered his voice to the same level, sensing something exciting was about to happen. Panos took down two dusty old tin mugs from a shelf and wiped them on his ragged old t-shirt. Then he bent down and turned the spigot of one of the giant barrels. The amber liquid made a pleasing gurgling sound as it spurted out, then settled down and slowly filled up one of the mugs. The strong smell of alcohol filled the musty air.

Panos set the mug down then filled the other one. He put his finger to his lips. 'You are old enough now. You are a man, not a word to your mother now,' he whispered as he handed Dimitri one of the wine-filled mugs.

'Stini Yamas! *Good health son.*'

'Yamas Papa.'

They clinked mugs together. Dimitri put his lips to the mug and took a small sip. He'd been allowed to taste it before at family celebrations, but only mixed with water. He watched his father put his own mug to his lips and take a large gulp of the home made wine.

'Kala eh?' Panos said.

'Very good Papa,' Dimitri replied.

Panos slapped his son good naturedly on the back. He replaced the empty mugs.

'Our secret eh son?' he whispered.

'Our secret Papa,' Dimitri smiled.

Panos and Dimitri were standing in the sunshine by the barbeque pit, taking it in turns to baste the lamb in its own juices. Both had striped blue and white aprons on. The heady scent of the lamb and rosemary and thyme filled the warm easter Sunday air.

Simon was the first to arrive as always. He had a thing about punctuality. He was greeted warmly by Eleni and Roula and offered a drink. He handed over a bag containing two bottles of wine and some beer to Eleni.

'Happy Easter everyone,' Simon said, as he walked over to the fire pit, beer in hand. Panos and Dimitri were busy. 'Hi guys, this looks great and smells great too, I can't wait, my mouth's watering.'

'Happy Easter,' a familiar voice called out.

'Happy Easter to you too Mags - It's lovely to see you. Let me get you a drink,' Eleni said.

'Good day Roula, nice to see you after so long,' Mags said. My you're growing up to be a fine young lady.'

Roula blushed and ran to help her mother prepare the drinks. Eleni came up to them and handed Mags her drink and they walked over to the fire pit and wished Panos and Dimitri a Happy Easter.

'Happy Easter everyone. Looks like we have a beautiful day for it,' said Panos, looking skywards and smiling broadly.

'Ah look Eleni, here's Giorgios and his family. It's been ages since we saw them.'

Georgios and his wife Katerina and their family came over to join the small band who had already arrived.

'Kalo Pascha Panos and Eleni.'

'Kalo Pascha Giorgios and Katerina.'

'What a day for it,' said Georgios.

'Perfect,' Panos replied.

By midday the garden of Panos and Eleni's house had filled with over forty friends and family. Panos and Dimitri sliced the cooked lamb with great ceremony and cut it into chunks and laid it on plates which were set out on trestle tables. He and Dimitri had brought over copious quantities of beer and wine earlier from his taverna across the road. *They certainly won't go without alcohol,* thought Simon, as he surveyed the scene. The garden was thronged with people, laughing and talking and eating and drinking. Panos finally took a break and came over to join Simon and Mags, who had been standing together.

'Well done mate,' Simon said. 'What a feast.'

'Yes you've done well Panos ma man,' said Mags, taking a drag of her cigarette. She passed Panos one. He took a large drink of his homemade wine and Mags lit his cigarette for him.

'Thank you my friends. I couldn't have done it all without Dimitri though.'

He called his son over. 'Ela Dimitri.'

Dimitri ambled over awkwardly and Panos put his arm around him and gave him a huge hug.

'I was just telling everyone what a great team we are eh.'

'Yes Papa, the best,' Dimitri replied, looking a little flushed.

'Hey, go easy on that homemade wine my boy. Remember we have all day to go.'

'Yes Papa.' He gave his father a lopsided grin.

'Kids eh,' he said, looking at Simon and Mags.

'Never lucky enough to have any myself,' said Mags, blowing some smoke skywards.

'Me neither,' replied Simon.

'A curse and a blessing,' said Panos.

Simon chewed on a large piece of lamb. This is delicious, it's falling off my fork.'

'Yes we were up from dawn, basting and slow cooking it. I'm pretty pleased with it.'

The celebrations carried on into the late afternoon and it became a little chilly. The women pulled shawls around them and the men put fleeces on. Panos was talking to a group of musicians he had hired for the day. They had various instruments and two of them had the traditional Greek Bouzouki. They began warming up, which caught everyone's attention and people gravitated naturally towards the sound of the music. Panos was the first up to dance. He was surprisingly nimble for such a heavy man. He swooped and jumped in the traditional Syrtaki dance, and his movements were at times balletic. Other men joined him and formed a line and began speeding up and each man tried to outdo the other, despite the advanced ages of some of them. The women soon followed, still keeping in their own groups at first, then facing the men, and allowing them the opportunity of showing off their moves. The men performed the *Belly Dance,* traditionally thought of as a women's dance - but in Greece it was the domain of the man. It was a sensuous dance - where the man woos his woman, and dances literally at her feet, as well as moving away and then facing her again - rhythmically turning and suggestively moving his hips. The hypnotic music played on, sensuous and exotic and people began clapping in time, as the dancers worked themselves into a frenzy of *Kefi* - the Greek trance-like state of bliss. Every time Panos and the other men leapt up and clapped their hands the crowd shouted *OPA!* and it encouraged the dancers to move even faster and try even more acrobatic moves. Simon and Mags had never seen Panos so animated and joyful in the way he danced. Eleni had now joined him and the couple moved together with a lightness of foot and grace, intertwined with a physical and erotic urgency - that left both of them exhausted when the music stopped. They fell into one another's arms smiling and took a bow - to thunderous applause and whooping, which filled the early evening air. The celebrations went on well into the night, until it was time to leave and Panos and Eleni waved off their guests into the chill night air.

4

MOTORBIKING

A few days later Simon was sitting in his lounge feeling restless. He was happy that his article about island life had been accepted and he put the money towards his house fund. He decided to have a day out and made up some lunch, then went down to his wooden garage and dragged his old rusty motorbike out of the shed and filled it with oil and petrol. Surprisingly, it started after a few attempts and blasted black smoke out of the exhaust, causing him to cough several times. He gunned the throttle several times and gradually increased his speed, as he took the main road into town, the hot wind on his face. He thought of the times he and Siobhan had driven across the island on a whim and remembered how she'd clung to him, her warm body pressed up against his. He headed through the harbour of Neo Horio, and up the hill and out to the narrow coast road, past the old monastery of Agia Epistoli, feeling the wind against his body, and savouring the freedom to please himself. The herby scent of thyme and oregano filled the warm countryside air.

He drove on, snaking through tiny old villages unchanged in centuries, passing dilapidated windmills, yellowed with age, that sat high up on the scorched red hillsides and he came to a halt above the perfect little scimitar - shaped bay of Orthi Ammos and turned off his engine. It felt so quiet after his noisy bike ride. The sea glittered below him, turquoise blue and glassy and calm as a pond. He heard the hiss of the small waves unravelling and breaking on the shore and the breath of the breeze in the fierce early afternoon sun. Then he walked down to the familiar pebble and sand beach and sat for a while and remembered. This was *their* spot, where they'd spent many lazy days, having picnics and bottles of wine, and making alfresco love, when they had the beach to themselves. He sat for a while gazing out to sea, the little offshore islands were clearer now that the haze was burning off. Then he peeled down to his shorts and rushed into the sea. The water was icy cold and made him gasp. The chill soon went and he swam freely into the waves, then he stood up, and splashed water on his face over and over, as if trying to cleanse himself of something and retraced his footsteps up the beach - and vigorously towelled himself dry and soon began to warm up again. The rucksack he'd brought with him contained some cheese and fresh bread and olives and he fished them out and laid them on his beach towel - then uncorked a bottle of white wine he'd kept in the fridge overnight and poured it into a plastic cup. It felt strange to be doing this on his own - it was the first time he'd been back here without her.

After a while he put his t-shirt and trainers on and picked up his rucksack and headed slowly back up the beach to collect his bike. He saw a figure coming towards him as he rounded the top of the beach near his motorbike. He recognised the eastern European woman from town. He thought to himself, *be cool man, be cool*. As they drew closer to one another he noticed that her shoulder length hair was wet and they both stopped.

'Morning, beautiful day, the water's still a bit cold though, still early in the season,'Simon said.

'Morning – yes, I've just been swimming in the little bay, I didn't stay in long. It's so quiet here, I do not think many tourists know about this spot. The locals must think I am mad, at this time of year.'

Simon smiled. 'The locals don't go near the water until June at least. You decided to stay on then?'

'Yes, I've rented a cottage a few miles from Ayia Varvara.'

'I know it, it's so quirky - the hippy dippy village we call it.'

'Yes - I'm on the outskirts though - it's quite remote - I don't have much company - but the solitude suits me at the moment, - but the few people I do see are very friendly...Anyway, it was nice to see you again. I'd better be going - I have things to do.' She smiled at him, and walked down the path towards a moped - which was parked against a fence.

'Bye then,' Simon replied, raising his arm to wave. He stole a glance as she walked away, noticing that her wet top clung to her body, outlining the curve of her hips.

He remembered an old friend who lived down the coast and on impulse decided to drive down and see her. His bike rounded the stunning bay of Agia Ekaterini and he reduced his speed so that he could enjoy looking at the azure sea. The sweat clung to his back and he soon saw a familiar little cottage up ahead and spotted Sophie in her front garden - she was watering some geraniums in colourful pots and he came to a halt and killed the engine - got off his bike and set it against her garden wall.

'Hi Sophie,' he waved over at her. She waved back and walked towards him and set the watering can down. He took at her tanned legs and her full figure, as she slowly walked towards him. He and Siobhan often drove down on the bike to this area and would sometimes stop by for a chat with Sophie. Siobhan and Sophie were kindred spirits and Siobhan knew he was attracted to her and had often teased him good naturedly about it. Jealousy was not one of Siobhan's traits. She believed people should be free.

She padded over to him and stooped slightly as she came out from under her porch, her tall frame stark against the midday shadows - and came up to him in her bare feet and gave him a lingering hug and a kiss on both cheeks. He smelt her perfume and faint scent of fresh sweat. She had a short hippy print dress on and a purple headband, that framed her thick blond sunkissed hair, that came down to her shoulders.

'Well...long time no see Simon McCardle. I heard you were back, but you know what it's like out here, we're so remote from everything. I was so sorry to hear about dear Siobhan - you must have been devastated. I was gutted.' She had a cut-glass English accent and it was rumoured that her family back in England were very wealthy.

Simon blinked in the sunlight. 'Yes, it was pretty tough. I can't believe it's been nearly a year. I guess life has to go on though, or is that too much of a cliche?'

'Of course not, but it must be hard for you,' Sophie said, tilting her head to one side.

He nodded and changed tack and pointed over to a pile of olive driftwood in the yard, some of it had been made into mirrors and children's chairs. She was clearly very talented. 'How's the business going, sold much?'

'Not bad this season, quite a few tourists stop by, it's the perks of living on such a small island. I have a website now so that helps,' she replied.

'Still doing your therapy stuff too?'

'Yes, that's getting busy. Not sure how I'll fit it all in. Do you want to come in for some home-made lemonade and get out of this heat?'

'Why not, I've got no other plans.' He followed her into the house and had to stoop down under the vine covered porch and he knocked his head against a set of giant wind chimes, which set them off clanging and tinkling.

'Oops sorry.'

She giggled. 'Don't worry everyone does that, I should really move them.'

'Have a seat.' Sophie pointed to a battered old chair that looked like something from the seventies. She went over to the fridge and took out a jug of her homemade lemonade and poured two glasses and sat down opposite him. He took a long drink and savoured the cold, zesty taste.

He stretched out his legs and crossed one foot over the other. 'Ahh, just the job.'

Sophie set down her glass...'I heard about the Ruthven thing. Hope you don't mind me mentioning it?'

'Jude told you I'll bet.'

She nodded. 'This is tiny Xanthos remember - not Crete.'

'Of course.' He took a slug of his lemonade. 'The Xanthos telegraph.'

'Indeed. Ruthven's always been a thoroughly obnoxious man. I've never liked him - Jude said he deserved it. I feel sorry for his poor wife.'

'He said some horrible things about Siobhan - bigoted bastard,' Simon said.

'He certainly is.'

Sophie took a long drink. 'Let's talk about nicer things... Siobhan and I got on so well, we had similar personalities I guess, a bit...alternative - for want of a better word.' She smiled. 'She was a bit off the wall, also like me I guess, not exactly one to follow the herd.'

'She was certainly all of that and a bit of a handful at times. I remember that time with you and her at the karaoke night at Max's bar. You did a duet of *Wild Thing*. I can see you both now. It was an amazing performance.'

Sophie smiled. 'That was a l o n g time ago - great memories though.'

Simon raised his glass. 'To happy times and many more to come I hope.'

'To happy times,' Sophie replied.

'Anyone special in your life at the moment?' Simon asked.

Sophie smiled...'Well...funny you should say that. I *have* been seeing someone for a little while.'

'Tell all,' he said, sitting forward in his chair.

'I guy I met through my business. He bought some of my stuff a few weeks ago and we kind of hit it off - an Italian, a bit younger than me - lives on his yacht, it's moored at Neo Horio - a bit of a nomad - like me. I guess that might be part of the attraction. He's sailing off into the sunset in a few weeks though, may be back, may not be. I kind of like that in a way. I've done the conventional stuff in the past and it never really worked and I love my freedom and hate being tied down. You know all this.'

'Yes of course. I know you and Siobhan were kindred spirits and I see how that might work for you. 'Maybe I could meet up for a drink with you and your new man sometime?'

'That sounds great. No guarantee he'll still be here though, he may have gone back to his other mistress - the sea.'

Simon drained his glass. 'Best be going - stuff to do.'

'I'll look forward to that drink,' Sophie said.

They walked out to the front garden. 'It's been great to see you again after all this time. Be happy. Siobhan would have wanted that.' She gave him a warm hug and kissed him on both cheeks.

He smiled. 'I know. Thanks for the chat, speak soon and we'll sort that drink out.'

5

AISHA

The coast road was very quiet - as he passed stunning little bays and whitewashed churches and spotted some garish tents on the beach, belonging to wild campers. He was approaching the bay where he'd swam and noticed a figure up ahead on the road and he slowed down. As he got closer he saw that it was the woman again. She was sitting on a moped, with her head down, looking a bit disconsolate. He came to a halt beside her, cut the engine and pulled up his bike stand.

'Need some help?'

She looked up, smiling broadly. 'Yes please, it won't start, it's my own fault, it was cheap, they saw the foreigner coming eh?' she smiled. and he noticed a gap in her front teeth.

'Maybe,' he said, smiling back.'It happens. 'Let's take a look.' He bent down and took the petrol cap off and peered inside the tank. Then he tried unsuccessfully to kick start it.'Plenty of petrol, could be the carburettor, it's an old bike. I can get someone to come and have a look tomorrow if you like?'

'That's kind, thank you.'

'Would you like a lift?'

'Yes please. - if it's not too much trouble.'

'It'll be safe here, no one will touch it, well unless they get it started of course. Just joking, the crime rate is very low here'

She smiled, then hopped on the back of his bike. He felt the warmth of her body - and drove off down the track that was signposted - with an old piece of driftwood - in bright colours; *Agia Varvara - Twinned with Narnia*. A few miles down the road he came to the small hamlet where she lived and she pointed out the house she was renting. She got off the bike and swept her long hair back and squinted in the afternoon sun.

'Thanks so much - it would have been quite a walk in this heat.'

'It's fine, my pleasure. I'm sorry I don't even know your name.'

'Aisha...Mihilovic,' she replied.

'Simon McCardle, nice to meet you,' he said, shaking her hand.

'Do you want to come in for, how do you English say, a cup of tea?'

'Well yes thank - you, but I'm Irish, well, Northern Irish actually. I'd prefer a coffee if you have it, thanks.'

'I wondered what your strong accent was.'

'It's not as strong as it once was. I left home when I was young.

He parked his bike and followed her into the house. It was small, painted white, quite old and built in the traditional island style and had a well-tended garden at the side. She pointed to a metal table and chairs. 'Have a seat.' and disappeared into the kitchen.

She returned with two cups of coffee and he caught her scent, as she leaned over - to hand him his coffee. She smelt of musky sweat and salt and the sea. He sipped his coffee and took in his surroundings. She crossed her tanned legs and he tried not to stare.

'I'm guessing you're not a tourist. How long have you lived here then Simon?'

'I've been coming here for over thirty years, on holiday, but I've been here nearly a year this time...My wife Siobhan and I were building a house... She died suddenly, nearly a year ago. I came back to finish the house. We were planning to move here permanently.'

She furrowed her brow. 'I'm so sorry, I didn't mean to upset you.'

'No need to apologise, you didn't know.' He took a sip of coffee and set his cup down.

Aisha had her head tilted to one side, her brown eyes looking at him intently and she brushed her thick dark hair away from her face.

'It must have been hard for you. Do you have children?'

'No, we never had children, too wrapped up in each other I guess.'

'So what are your plans now? You said that you're a writer. I love words, you must write something about this beautiful island of yours.'

'I've written some stuff about Xanthos recently, funnily enough, for a tourist website.'

'I'd like to read it?' She stood up slowly and beckoned him with her finger. 'Come, come see my garden.'

He followed her through into a little courtyard and watched a damp trickle of sweat running down her back as she walked. She had a tiny walled garden, with huge terracotta pots filled with spiky agave and grasses. A small vegetable patch had carrots, onions and some lime green melons were ripening in the red earth. The air was filled with the herby scent of oregano, mixed with pungent onion.

'This is impressive.'

'Thank you, but I can't take all the credit, most of them were already planted by the time I arrived. I grow stuff back home though.'

'You're a long way from home.'

'I'm here for a holiday,' she explained brightly..

'You were meant to go to Athens, on the ferry, you must like it here?'

'You're still asking a lot of questions I see.'

'It's my job, or rather it was my job. I was a journalist. So...you liked our little island and decided to stay for a while?'

'Are you hungry? I've not eaten since breakfast. Swimming always makes me hungry.'

'I am a bit - thanks.'

'Unless you have other plans?'

'I don't make many plans these days.'

They sat at the little blue dining table in the kitchen on two wickerwork chairs and ate grilled lamb chops - baby potatoes and a feta cheese and tomato salad .

'That was delicious,' he said, as he wiped his mouth with his napkin and took a generous slug of his wine.

'Thank you. It's nice to cook for someone. Come into the lounge - it's cooler.'

They both sat close together on a little patterned hippy - print couch. Her arm brushed against his.

'So, you know *my* background, what do *you* do for a living?'

'I lecture in history - at the University of Sarajevo.'

'That sounds interesting.'

'It is - but I've been doing it for a long time now. I'm thinking of changing careers, maybe try teaching yoga. I've done some courses. I'd like to do something a bit more spiritual.'

'When do you go back to work then?'

'When I said holiday...I actually meant I'm on a Sabbatical. I was in Crete for a while, visiting Knossos and other ancient sites and I headed to Athens to see some more. The stop off wasn't planned of course.'

'Of course, one of these things,' he said, before continuing. 'Is January not an unusual time to be travelling. It's not the best weather?'

'It was a last minute thing. I've been through a bit of a difficult time recently. It affected my job. I was signed off sick for a while. I wasn't going to mention it, but you seem to be a good listener. I had a bit of a tough time, around the date of Mladic's trial in November last year. I'm sure that it wasn't a coincidence. You wouldn't think it would still bother me after all these years, but my doctor said it's quite common after witnessing traumatic events.'

'That sounds like a type of Post Traumatic Stress Disorder to me,' he said, sympathetically.

'Yes you are correct. She said it was because I'd been through the siege of Sarajevo and we also heard about the terrible Srebrenica massacre and saw the aftermath on television. I lived in Sarajevo during the war, for the four years it lasted. I think it all came back to me. I felt overwhelmed and I was signed off work. I found out later that many of my colleagues and friends and family also suffered with the condition around the same time. It brought it all back to you see, even though people celebrated the Butcher Mladic finally being sentenced. The other Butcher of Bosnia, Karadzic, had been sentenced in 2016, so people got a double dose of it - all the memories re-surfaced.'

'I remember Srebrenica now - dreadful. It must have been terrible to relive it all again.'

She nodded and dabbed at her eyes with a tissue. 'I wish for them both to burn in hell and all the other monsters.'

She walked into the kitchen and opened some more wine - then walked unsteadily back and re-filled their glasses.

'You are very easy to talk to.'

'So are you Aisha - tell me more about your job situation.'

'The University kindly agreed to give me a year's paid sabbatical, as long as I did some research related to my job. I planned to get back on the ferry, but something inside me said no, it's peaceful here on this little island, so it felt right to stay here, for a while anyway - so here I am.'

She reached over and pulled some more tissues out from her bag and wiped her eyes, then blew her nose loudly.

'What must I look like?'

'You look lovely.' He held her hand and squeezed it gently. She leaned forward and he kissed her and she responded. He started to kiss her neck and she moaned softly.

***

The early morning sun filtered into the bedroom through the gaps in the blue shutters. For a moment he hadn't a clue where he was. Then he turned around and his face rubbed against her shoulder and he remembered, then relaxed, and kissed her gently on her back and wrapped his arm around her. She turned around to face him.

'Sorry, did I wake you?' he mumbled.

'Well I don't think we had much sleep anyway,' she smiled.

'You surprised me, in lots of ways,' he said.

'I surprised myself?' she brushed her hair from her eyes, and moved closer to him. 'I can see you are a sensitive man. Oh and just for the record. I don't usually jump into bed with a man I've just met.'

He smiled. 'I'm sure you don't, but we're both adults.'

'Thank you for listening last night. It really did help. I was meaning to ask you about your own life, but got a bit caught up with my own stuff, sorry.'

'No need to be sorry. I was brought up in Belfast, during the time they called the Troubles.'

'I remember seeing it on the news as a young girl growing up - the IRA and the British Army.'

'Yes, I'm not comparing it to Sarajevo, but it was a horrible time to be growing up, what with all the shootings and the bombings and road blocks. I left as soon as I could and went to work in London. I'll tell you about it some time if you'd like.'

'I'd like that...very much.'

6
THE DRIVE BACK

He drove back towards Neo Chorio in the late - morning sunlight and he felt happy for the first time in a long time. The locals were up and about as he drove through the little villages that dotted the coast, sweeping outside their doorways and getting ready for the day. Elderly ladies in black scarves headed into the fields on donkeys and he slowed down to let them pass, and received a Good Morning here and there.

'Kalimera, Kalimera,' he replied. The old men sat outside the Kafenion on basketwork chairs and smoked and waved as he drove by. His Greek had improved since he moved back to the island. It was a beautiful language and he enjoyed speaking it. He loved the island people and friends like Panos and Eleni. He reached Neo Chorio and drove past the harbour and up the hill and pulled into Panos's taverna. It was filling up with tourists for a coffee or an early lunch. The early May sun was already fierce and the flowers were colourful and abundant in the little garden bordering the taverna.

'Bloody hell, where have *you* been! I have been looking for you. I phoned loads of times.' Panos bellowed across the taverna, as he saw his friend approach, oblivious to the customers who turned around to have a better look at this little scene unfolding.

'Turned my mobile off mate, bad reception,' he said - as he got closer to his friend.

The taverna was decorated in its finery, colourful Flokati rugs adorned the walls, along with old guns and black and white photographs of Panos's family, stretching back several generations. In the older photos, the men stood proudly, with stern faces, and all wore fierce black moustaches. The unsmiling women wore black head scarves and looked equally severe. The warm air held the tangy scent of thyme and of barbecued lamb and waiters bustled busily among the customers, setting down trays of delicious food and setting tables for the busy tourist lunchtime.

'Give us a beer please mate. I'm thirsty.'

Panos shouted at one of the young waiters to bring drinks, then walked up to Simon and shook his hand warmly. 'You been hiding eh?' he smiled broadly.

'Something like that,' Simon replied, as he sat down at a table..

'Well tell me then, who is she?

'Dunno what you mean, I just needed to get away. I've only been gone for a day.'

'Ha, of course you did, so who is she?' he repeated. 'I know you too well. You have met someone.'

The waiter set down Simon's beer and he took a long drink, aware that Panos was beside himself with curiosity.

Simon pointed behind Panos and said, 'You've got some customers, mate, better go and look after them.'

He frowned.'I'll be back, don't go away.' He walked over to greet the tourists, and went into full charm mode. Simon overheard him.

'Welcome to the best taverna on Xanthos. You have made a good choice, come sit down and enjoy. The specials today are sea bream, sardines, and Stifado.' He pointed at the blackboard, and carried on explaining the menu. He scuttled back to where Simon was sitting as soon as he could and sat down and leaned forward over the table and whispered.

'Now you must stop with this, put me out of my misery. Where have you been? Eleni said maybe you have met up with the foreign woman, but I said no way, she is too angry to talk to men. Beautiful, but cold, No?'

Simon smiled again, he was enjoying this, it was like playing a fish on a hook.

He drained the last of his beer, and stood up. Look mate - I've been away for a little while to sort my head out and now I feel better - there's no mystery - no woman, nothing - you nosey bugger. Now go and look after your customers.' He slapped Panos on the back and smiled and began to walk out the taverna. Eleni was behind the bar.

'Hi.' Eleni waved at him, and he winked at her as he passed.

It was later that afternoon when a knock came to the door. Simon opened it and he wasn't surprised.

'Eleni says I am too nosey - I am to give you some, how do you say, space, no?' 'Ha, she's right, space, that's what we all need, come in mate.'

'I worry about you, you've been gone for a while.'

'Only one day - like I said - I needed to get away.'

'I understand, but still worry,'

'Thanks for your concern, but I'm ok. Would you like a beer?'

'Coffee thanks."

He returned with two coffees and two small glasses of water.

'Ok. It *was* that woman, Eleni was right.' Simon confessed.

'The foreign woman, the angry one?'

'The angry one, yes.'

'Bloody hell, you kept that quiet. She is beautiful. You dirty dog.'

'I met her on the beach, the one that Siobhan and I used to go to - you remember?

'Agia Ekaterina? I saw her there ages ago when I was fishing with my cousin. Eleni said she told you.'

'Yes Eleni mentioned you'd seen her. But that was a while back. She was there, she'd been swimming.' He took a sip of his coffee. 'We got talking, then she had to go. I drove down the coast to see Sophie, the artist, you know her.'

'Of course,' Panos said.

'Well, on the way back I noticed the woman standing by the side of the road, where I'd left her. Her moped wouldn't start. I gave her a lift and then she invited me to her house for a cup of tea.'

'Tea, is that what they call it now?' Panos roared with laughter.

Simon smiled. 'Well there's a bit more to it.'

'I thought so - I mean why was she staying there - when she was on the way to Athens?' he enquired.

'Exactly, I thought the same. It's to do with the conflict in the Balkans many years ago. She's from Bosnia and Herzegovina. She's going through a bit of a hard time - memories and stuff. She needed a holiday and liked it here because of the peace and quiet.'

Panos lit a cigarette and leaned back in his chair.

'You've been through a lot recently yourself my friend,' Panos said sympathetically. 'You don't have to fall in love with her though, just enjoy, you deserve some happiness. But please be careful.' Panos put his hand on his chest, 'with your heart.'

Simon nodded.

'You must both come for dinner tomorrow night, it's on me.'

He woke early, he hadn't really slept that well - with all the stuff in his head, although he managed to put a little perspective on things. It looked like she was here for a while anyway, so why didn't he take his friend's advice and just go with the flow? She'd probably be gone at the end of the Summer anyhow. He showered and had some toast and coffee and decided to give her a ring. She sounded pleased to hear from him and it was good to hear her voice again.

'Hi, I'm glad you called,' she said brightly. I'm just about to go into town for some supplies. Do you want to meet for coffee?'

'Yes great, what time?'

'Around eleven at the little café by the bank?'

'Ok see you then,' said Simon.

She was already seated outside when he arrived. She had a long red and black dress on, which revealed her brown shoulders. He lent over to kiss her on the neck, and she turned her head and he smelt the scent of her again, a mixture of sweat, perfume and coconut oil.

He sat down. 'How's things?'

'Ok. I'm still trying to come to terms with what I told you I suppose, maybe I shouldn't have…you know dumped it on you. We've only just met. You've been through enough yourself with your poor wife.'

'You trusted me enough to offload to me. And besides, it's not good to keep that stuff to yourself,' he replied.

She reached across the table and touched his arm. 'Thank you, you're kind.'

He reached over to gently touch her cheek.

'People will talk,' she giggled.

'Let them,' he said. 'They will anyway, nothing much is missed on this little island.'

'I'm sure it's not.'

'Shall we take a walk?' he suggested.

They finished their coffees and she took his hand and they began to walk down a little cobbled alleyway. They slowed down as they reached an old whitewashed building - Its arched doorway was studded with iron, and the wood was bleached and split from centuries of sun and wind and salty air. They stopped and he kissed her and she responded. They heard some people coming down the street towards them and stopped and walked over and sat down on a low wall in Eleftherios Square at the back of town, a large fountain stood in the middle and the water provided a cooling breeze in the midday heat.

'So what's your plans then?' he asked.

'I've not thought too far ahead, maybe stay here for a while. My work has been very good about it all.'

He smiled at her reassuringly and her gaze lingered on his pale blue eyes.

'What about your family back home?'

'My mother and younger sister and older brother. I miss them of course.'

'Do they know what you're going through?'

'Yes, we are a close family, the war made us closer too. They too have suffered. It was they who suggested I take this holiday.'

Simon thought she looked like she was gazing into the distance, as if to try and connect with her family hundreds of miles away.

'Homesick?' he asked.

'Good guess. Of course, but I needed this break.'

'No one special to go back home to, apart from your family?'

'I told you - you ask too many questions Mr Irish.' She blinked in the strong sunlight.

His confident smile returned. 'Yes, sorry. It's the journalist in me.'

'No, not right now, but there was someone. I've had a few relationships since, but no one special.'

'I see.'

'Panos said I should just enjoy your company and not think of tomorrow.'

'Did he now? Well maybe you can tell your lecher friend, he is not so stupid after all?'

'You can tell him yourself - he's invited us to dinner tonight at his taverna. I mean if you're free that is?'

She considered it for a moment and smiled. I...shall have to check my social diary, you know how it is?'

He smiled. 'Of course, but if you do, I'll tell him to be on his best behaviour, besides, Eleni will be there.'

'His wife? don't worry. I can look after myself.'

'I do believe that you can.'

7

A NIGHT AT THE TAVERNA

The place was noisy when Simon and Aisha arrived. A slight breeze ruffled the taffeta leaves of the palm trees surrounding the taverna. It was full of tourists and some locals too. The familiar strains of popular Greek music rang out into the warm night air, mingling with the fragrant smells of lamb and fish cooking on the charcoal grill. A clutch of piratical looking skinny cats skittered about looking for food, some had only one eye, others with battle-scarred ears. Panos and Eleni and their staff were buzzing around, setting tables and serving meals and drinks, glasses and plates were clinking, amidst the hum of conversation from customers speaking several different languages. They were predominantly German and British, with a smattering of Scandinavians and some Eastern Europeans and of course the locals, who liked to eat late. They were easy to spot by their good natured exuberance and always sounded to the untrained ear as if they were arguing. Simon took Aisha's hand as they walked under the vine-canopied roof and they walked over to a table already set up for them, reserved in the usual way with an unopened bottle of wine.

'You look stunning,' he whispered in her ear.'

'Thank you,' Aisha smiled. 'You scrub up pretty well yourself, as she tugged at his white linen shirt. You smell nice.'

'Thank you Ma'am.' He pulled out a chair for her, and she sat down.

Panos waved over to them, and motioned for *two minutes* with his fingers. Simon waved back. One of the young waiters took their drinks orders.

At last Panos bustled over to their table, looking slightly harassed, smoothing down his blue polo shirt and he stood to attention, then bowed his head. 'Good evening, welcome.'

'Hi mate.' Simon shook hands, and then he gestured to his left. 'This is Aisha, I believe you two have seen each other before,' he added mischievously.

It had the desired effect. Panos looked suitably embarrassed and then he extended his hand to Aisha. 'Very pleased to meet you Aisha. Welcome to our little island, and to my taverna.'

'Thank you,' Aisha replied. 'It's a very beautiful island. How long have you had this place?'

'Ah, let me think, my grandfather opened it just after the civil war, so we have been here for nearly seventy years. Not me personally of course,' he said, smiling. 'It was much smaller then of course. I have some photographs.' He pointed over to a wall near the bar, covered in family photos through the ages. 'I will show you later if you like.'

'Thank you, I would like that.'

'My pleasure,' He said. 'Aisha, what a lovely name.'

'Thank you. I am sure that your wife has a lovely name too. I can see from here that she is very beautiful, you are a very lucky man.'

'Yes, Yes - my lovely Eleni. I am lucky, of course I am, we are devoted to one another. Now...what would you like to eat? I can recommend the Kleftiko, or we have special fresh sardines in garlic from the grill, caught today by my cousin.'

Simon was sitting back, silently enjoying it all unfolding in front of him. Panos took their orders and with a conspiratorial wink to his friend, he scuttled off to the kitchen.

A waiter soon brought over a myriad of tiny plates - glossy black olives slicked with oil and garlic and a selection of snacks, tiny pieces of cured ham, blood red sliced tomatoes, tiropita - little cheese pies, thick creamy hummus, hot pitta bread, pink taramasalata, and tzatziki - full of tangy yoghurt with cucumber and zingy garlic, and melitzano salata - small pieces of grilled aubergine in vinegar and garlic and a pot of black olive tapenade and mashed fava beans. It was a delight for the senses, and they picked over the little snacks until the plates were empty. Panos came back in about half an hour, full of apologies, carrying a large tray of food.

'Sorry, we are very busy tonight, the tourists you know.'

'Not complaining then?' Simon joshed.

'Of course not - I just want to serve my friends a good meal, on the house of course.'

'The meze was delicious Panos, what a cook you must have.' Aisha complimented him.

'Eleni, the best cook in Greece, and the prettiest. She'll be over in a minute to say hello. She's looking forward to meeting you Aisha. - Ahh... and here she is.'

Elenis came to the table, looking a bit flustered.. She wiped her hands on the apron and shook hands with Aisha. 'Hi Aisha, how lovely to meet you. Evening Simon. I'm sorry I wasn't able to come over sooner - we are so busy - as you can see. We'll all have a drink later when it quietens down a bit.'

Panos set down the main courses - sardines and kleftiko, grilled lamb and a bowl of small, sweet potatoes, dressed in butter and rosemary, some fresh olive bread and a huge bowl of Greek Salad. The salty, whitewashed cubes of feta sat atop fresh slices of cucumber, onions, black olives and green peppers, and voluptuous, blood red aromatic tomatoes, drizzled in the island's pungent virgin olive oil. The ingredients were sprinkled with fresh oregano and other herbs from his own garden. It smelled delicious, and the aroma of garlic and lamb, and olive oil suffused the warm night air. He came back and proudly placed a large carafe of amber wine in front of them and two small glasses.

'I made this myself.' He beamed at Aisha. 'Enjoy your meal.'

Panos hurried away to greet more customers and later, after sweet almond filled baklava, and a plate of fresh plums and quinces, they both sat back and sighed contentedly. Aisha looked over at him as she dabbed her mouth with a linen napkin. 'That was absolutely delicious.'

'Eleni's a great cook.'

'She certainly is.'

The plates were cleared away and a waiter brought across a bottle of five star Metaxa brandy and two glasses - courtesy of Panos of course.

Simon's new relationship - so soon after Siobhan, had led to Panos telling Simon that Eleni was a bit worried. He reminded his friend that his wife had been very close to Siobhan. Panos told him that Eleni had talked about how the traditional Greek period of mourning was not as strictly observed as in previous generations and even in these more enlightened times, a widower could move on more quickly than a widow, and make a new relationship - if he was discreet about it. However old traditions die hard, and this particular one was still woven into the fabric of Greek culture; as traditional as the stitching on a Flokati rug. Simon had made a point of reminding his old friend that he was not of course Greek, but did appreciate and understand he and Eleni's worries and that he would be careful and take things slowly.

All the customers had gone, and the waiters were clearing up. Panos and Eleni came over and sat down. Panos sighed wearily, and set down a bottle of Johnie Walker whisky and poured some large measures out for everyone. He left Simon and Eleni to chat and then beckoned Aisha over to the wall, with all the photos of his family, past and present.

'This is Papa,' he said, pointing at an older version of himself. The photo had been taken inside the taverna, near the bar area, where they were now standing. How old was your father in this photo?' she enquired.

Panos stroked his beard. 'Seventy, maybe a bit older.' He looked wistful.

'He worked here until he dropped.'

'You must miss him,' she added.

'Every day,' he replied softly. 'But…life must go on,' he added.

'Of course,' she agreed. 'And…is this your Mama?' She pointed correctly at another photo, this time his mother and father stood together, looking proud, arms linked, smiling awkwardly for the camera.

'She was a lovely looking woman, Panos and he was a handsome man. He nodded and smiled. 'They were in love until the end…until the end.' He frowned, "Papa was a hard man though. He drove me and my brothers hard too, we worked in the taverna almost as soon as we could walk.'

Aisha nodded and continued listening. 'Your brothers, where are they now?'

'One is in America, New York, a very rich and successful man. He owns a fruit import business. He has a big house with a swimming pool and has done well. My other brother owns a big hotel in Rhodes.'

'What's their names?'

'Dimitri - named after my grandfather, and Georgios. Here is my grandfather, 'he said, pointing toward a photo of a taller older man, with an impressive beard and you could see the resemblance.

'My brothers left the island as soon as they could, to make their way.

'And do you see them at all, do they visit?'

'Dimitri - last time was four years ago. He is so far away, but I miss him of course. I miss Giorgios too, but I see him more often.'

Panos told Aisha about the visits he would regularly make to the little stonewalled graveyard, set on the hill above the town. He always placed flowers on his parents and grandparents' graves. He told her about how he would have conversations with his parents and let them know how the business was going, how much profit they had made and how their grandchildren were coming along. Generations of his family were buried here and Eleni's too. 'One day we will all go here - just like them - to be with God.'

'You're a deep thinking man I think, Panos.'

'Sometimes I think too much,' he replied, tapping his head.

'Not always the joker then?'

'I think maybe you found me out, Aisha.' he smiled. 'Do not tell anyone, or they will think Panos has gone soft.'

'Our secret.' She held out her hand.

'Of course,' he said, shaking solemnly on the deal.

She moved a bit closer to him, and touched his arm. 'I am sorry Panos - I want to apologise for being rude earlier. I got the wrong impression of you. I should not have judged so quickly. You are a good man.'

'Thank you, but I should not be looking.' He pointed his finger towards one eye, and smiled.

'Your mother and father would be very proud of you if they could see what a success you've made of their taverna, I'm sure…and of your friendship with Simon. You help him a lot - he told me you two are close and he said that he confided in you and Eleni about my situation,' she said.

'Of course - we're friends, your conversations are safe with us,' he assured her, warmly.

'Thank you.'

'What you see is what you get with Simon. He is a genuine man, a good man.' Panos assured her.

'I've been welcomed here so much by strangers. I am very touched Panos.'

'We have a word for it…*Xenos*, it means stranger and it also means friend or guest. It's an ancient tradition in Greece about offering hospitality to the stranger, who then becomes the friend. A stranger is only a friend that you have not met.'

'That wonderful, I love that,' she replied.

'We will look after you - don't worry. We are *Palikari*.' He flexed his right arm revealing a huge bicep and laughed out loud.

Aisha laughed along with him and Simon and Eleni looked over as their joy echoed through the near empty taverna.

'What does that mean?' she said when she had recovered.

'Palikari? We are warriors!' he said, as he beat his chest with his right hand.

'Oh Panos, you are so funny,' she said as she hugged him warmly. They returned to the table still laughing.

'Well - you two seem to be getting on well together,' Simon remarked, with a smile.

'Yes, we couldn't help but notice,' Eleni agreed, grinning 'They nearly heard you in Athens,' she joked.

'I think my wife is now the comedian Aisha,' Panos replied. Then he leant over and kissed Eleni.

It was the early hours now and Panos and Eleni said goodnight to their staff, leaving the taverna eerily quiet, apart from the rhythmic chirping of the cicadas and the distant hum of ubiquitous mopeds. The Johnnie Walker bottle was three quarters empty now, as were several jugs of Panos's home-made wine.

'Where did *you* two meet then?' Aisha asked Eleni

'We are both from the same village, just outside Neo Chorio, we grew up together, it happens on small islands' she explained.

'Yes, it's the same in Bosnia, the world over I suppose,' Aisha replied.

'It must be amazing to grow up and live on such a beautiful island.'

'I know, we are *very* lucky,' Eleni agreed, as she took Panos hand and they smiled at one another.

'We are both blessed with a great life and each other,' Panos said. 'Maybe *you* can have a great life too.

'I'm very grateful for the friendship you've all given me - and for treating me like, how did you say... Xenos?'

Eleni set down her glass, and looked at Aisha with kind eyes. 'It must have been such a terrible time for you growing up. Simon explained a little to us. The terrible war in your country did not touch us - of course we saw on the news, but it didn't affect us in that way. I hope that doesn't sound uncaring or selfish - but we seem so far away from the world here.'

'No, I understand,' Aisha said calmly. 'Bosnia is only a few hundred miles from here, but a million miles away in other ways.'

'What was it like living through that time?' Panos enquired softly. 'Unless it upsets you to talk?'

'I'm fine about it, just now and then, it can affect me of course. Do you really want to know?' she added.

'Of course,' Panos replied, lighting a cigarette.

Aisha drank some of her wine... 'The siege of my city, of Sarajevo, lasted four years. At first we thought it would only last a few months, but they.... the Serbians dug into the hillsides with heavy weapons and invaded the city. The noise of the shelling was terrifying, babies, children crying day and night, people screaming in fear of their lives. The smell of the explosives, the smoke, the fires, the noise. It was deafening. You never got used to it, no matter how many times you heard it. They blocked all the roads and shut down the airport. There were forty thousand of us trapped in the siege. Thousands were killed and wounded, friends, relatives, strangers. They raped women and young girls. They held mass executions.' She sounded so matter of fact, as if she had told this story a hundred times. Simon, Eleni and Panos listened, with horrified fascination.

'They destroyed or damaged every building. No one was safe from attack. One day fifteen people were killed and eighty were wounded from a mortar attack during a soccer game. Red Cross trucks brought us aid, but they were raided and destroyed. Then they bombed the maternity wards, killing mothers and newborn babies. People were killed while they waited in line for water or shopped in the market. We pretended life was normal - how crazy was that?

'We used to run across the town squares and open streets - dodging the snipers. I saw many people gunned down in front of me, including little children.

'How did you survive? I mean food and stuff, running water? Eleni asked.

'They cut off our food, medicine, water, and electricity, they tried to starve us to death - and we probably would have starved, if it wasn't for the United Nations airlifts from Sarajevo Airport. We still had very little food, people scavenged what they could. When we were unable to buy fresh food, people ate cats, dogs, rats, anything to stop them from starving.'

'Some people did crazy things. I remember one Christmas time...a musician, a famous musician - he climbed on top of a huge pile of rubble - it was what left of a building that had been bombed. It was so dangerous, but he climbed up anyway and began to play his clarinet. He performed a song about Sarajevo at Christmas, it was so emotional. Everyone came out of their homes to cheer him and those bastards shot at him, at *us* and tried to kill us...at Christmas. Can you believe it? That's how evil they were. They never won though....we would not bow down to them - ever.'

Eleni came to Aisha's side, and put her arm around her and passed her some tissues and Aisha dabbed her eyes and regained her composure.

'Sorry, so sorry - It just comes out sometimes.'

'No need to explain - we asked you to talk - you're among friends - it's better to let it out,' Panos said softly.

Aisha managed a weak smile. 'Thank you. Friends - Xenos - I remember.'

'Xenos,' repeated Panos and he raised his glass. 'Stini Yamas! Good health to us all and to better days for you Aisha - and for *you* also my friend.' he said looking at Simon. To you both.'

Eleni joined in. 'To better days and happiness for you both.'

8
THE HOUSE IN THE OLIVE GROVE

They had stayed the night at Panos and Elenis' house next to the taverna, as it turned out to be a very late one. Saturday was always a busy day but at least their kids didn't need to go to school. Simon padded across the cool marble floor to the windows and slowly opened the wooden shutters, letting the strong sunlight pour into the room.

Aisha stirred in the big double bed. 'What time is it?' she yawned, and stretched her legs out, pushing the covers off.

'Just after ten,' Simon replied. 'Jeeze, what the hell were we drinking?' he said, holding his head.

'You were drinking anything Panos poured out for you.'

'And I suppose *you* were on the holy water?' he smiled.

'No, I drank as much as you. It was a great night though. Sorry for being so emotional.'

'Don't be silly, you were fine. I told you - you have to let it out sometimes and as Panos said, you were among friends,' he added reassuringly.

'You have such lovely friends,' she replied.

'You're right. I don't know what I'd do without them. I'm sure you have some great friends back home too.'

'Yes I do,' replied Aisha,' I miss them.'

He walked slowly over to the bed and leant down and kissed her. She put her arms around his neck and pulled him down towards her.

'Come back to bed.'

He slid in the bed beside her and he felt the early morning warmth and sleepiness of her and he smelled her musky scent, as he began to kiss her and felt her eager response.

***

It was nearly 11 o'clock when Panos knocked tentatively on the door. 'Anyone alive in there?' he boomed. And they heard him chuckle 'Hello you two lovers, it's not siesta time yet.'

'Bugger off, we're tired!' Simon shouted. The door slowly opened as Panos knocked again several times, before tentatively entering the room.

'I have coffee for you.' He held a tray in his hands with two blue mugs of tea, and set it down by the bedside table. Aisha pulled the bedclothes further up and Simon sat upright.

'Thanks mate, just the job. Great night last night, that meal was amazing - thanks so much.'

'It was Eleni, not me,' Panos replied modestly, trying to avert his gaze from Aisha.

'Thanks Panos, it was a wonderful night and thank you also for your and Eleni's friendship. I'm so lucky,' Aisha added.

'No problem, Simon's friend is *our* friend, and besides, you are good for him, you make him smile, he's not smiled in a long time.' Panos looked at his friend.

'Anyway I must go over to the taverna and look after my customers - I'm running late already. Please come and have some lunch before you leave. Are you going to show Aisha your new house by the way?'

'You read my mind mate,' Simon replied. 'Do you want to see it?'

'I'd love to, of course - thank you,' she replied.

'See you two later, be good.' Panos smiled at them and left the room.

'See you later mate.'

After they'd showered they popped into the Taverna for some lunch - then they caught a taxi up to Simon's house.

'Wow, what amazing views,' Aisha enthused, as the taxi climbed to the top of the hill overlooking the harbour.

'Wait 'til you see the even better views from my house, not far to go now,' Simon replied proudly

The taxi rounded the top of the hill and drove a few more hundred yards to Simon's house. It was another hot day and a light breeze rustled the cypress trees. He paid the taxi driver and took Aisha's hand and led her to the front of the house. It was set back from the road. She gazed up admiringly.

'It's so lovely. I see why you wanted to live here,' permanently,' she said, touching , touching the walls.

'Maybe I still will,' he replied enigmatically. 'Come inside.'

They walked into a large hallway. Aisha's eyes were drawn to a circular wooden table. There was a large silver - framed photo of a much younger Simon and an attractive young woman, who must of course have been Siobhan. It was taken at a beach - with a taverna in the background.

'May I?' Aisha asked, touching the photo frame... 'Of course,' he replied.

Aisha picked it up. There were some words typed on a piece of paper, underneath the photo.

Remembering a Xanthos Summer
The whispering Aegean wind, olive leaves dancing in the afternoon haze
The hum of chirruping cicadas as they whiled away their sunkissed days
Soft breezes ruffled an azure sea
We sat on a bleached barren rock you and me

I see you emerging from the salty brine
Rivulets of water on your sun brown body, sandy footprints made a line
You kissed me and I recall the musky coconut oil scent of you
And soon amidst the dunes we lay and discovered love anew

The harbour café that sleepy sunlit day, you and I watched the world go by
A shared Greek salad salty feta, the warm touch of your sunburnt thigh
The moped trip to the blue domed church a picnic on the holy mount
Nights of Greek dancing and days too heady and too crazy to keep count

There are photos of that summer somewhere, hidden in a lonely sheaf
But time can be a wily foe and time can be a thief
And the world turns as it always will and was forever thus
But time will never dim the sacred memory that once was us

Aisha carefully replaced the photo. She took a tissue out of her bag and dabbed her eyes. 'What simply beautiful words. She was a stunning looking young woman. And you both look so young.'

'I wrote it not long after she died. The photo was taken the year after we got married. The beach is Damnoni, it's down the South of the island.'

Aisha walked over and put her arms around him. 'Are you ok?'

'Yes, fine thanks. I have my moments. I should probably move that.

Some people might think it looks like a bit of a shrine - a bit morbid maybe?'

'I think it's a lovely way to remember your Siobhan.'

'Thank you.' He kissed her head.

He gave her a tour. She smelled the new plaster and paint and the varnish from the wooden beams. She told Simon that she was impressed by the balcony of the master bedroom, which had breathtaking views over the harbour and beyond, - to the offshore islands of Mathriki and Orthonoss.

'Does anyone live on those little islands?' she asked, pointing out to sea.

'A few people, but a lot more return in Summer, mainly from Australia strangely enough, where their families emigrated, years ago. It really swells the population. They all come back here eventually though, to retire...and to die of course.'

'Really? Well I can think of worse places. We all have to die I suppose,' she replied.

'Not for a very long time I hope,' he said, taking her hands in hers and kissing her forehead. She slipped her arms around his waist and they both gazed out to sea, enjoying the shared silence and the warmth of their bodies. Simon felt peaceful and content. Could he call it love? Whatever it was, he decided that he liked it and that he would live in the moment, just for this one time in his life and would surrender to whatever came his way. He felt at home here, that he somehow belonged. He didn't try to analyse it, take it apart and examine it, as he'd had done so many times in the past. He simply wanted to *be,* to sit in that space that he occupied right now. People sometimes said that the world stood still - that's how it felt right now and it was so warm and peaceful and good and calm and loving.

He led her down to the garden in the warm, late morning sunshine. A whisper of breeze gently ruffled the olive trees.

'This is amazing, just amazing. Look at these olive trees, there must be hundreds. And I love that old olive press. What a beautiful garden you have. I've run out of words.'

He smiled and pulled her close to him. 'Thanks, I love it all too and I'm getting used to living here. I was definitely going to sell it, but...' his voice trailed off.

'No you must keep living here, it suits you, it's so peaceful. Have you a name for it yet?' she asked.

'Name? Never thought of that.'

'Can I suggest one?'

'Of course, what did you have in mind?'

She thought for a moment. 'I know it sounds corny and a bit obvious -

but here goes. 'The house in the olive grove.' She looked at him doubtfully as he considered it.

'The house in the olive grove,' he repeated. 'Yes I like it. That's it, that's it,' he said, taking her in his arms and kissing her.

9

THE BOAT TRIP

The next few days were spent helping Aisha move her small amount of belongings into Simon's house. They'd decided this one night on the spur of the moment. He thought to himself, i*f it didn't work out, then so be it, but it just felt the right thing to do*. She had started working at Panos's taverna and was enjoying it and she was good at chatting with the customers and very efficient.

Simon was sitting at the taverna one day in June, just watching the world go by. It was a quiet period and Aisha came over and sat down. They had talked about her going back home to see her family.

'So it's agreed, you should go back for a while,' said Simon.

'Yes I'd like that,' replied Aisha 'I can't believe I've been here for so long, it's flown by,' she said.

'Me neither.' replied Simon. 'When are you thinking of going?'

'In about three weeks,' she replied. 'I have to organise ferries and flights.'

'Good, so you won't miss Panos's boat trip.'

'Boat trip?'

'Yes it's an annual event and we're invited. I've been to a few over the years - it's a brilliant day out. Panos gets his cousin's family to take over the taverna for the day and evening and it gives them a break. They work so damn hard over the season, they deserve a rest.

'Sounds great, I can't wait.'

***

The long awaited Saturday morning arrived, and with it came the promise of another searingly hot July day, with azure skies and just a whisper of a cooling breeze. Panos was already down at the quayside with Eleni Roula and Dimitri, loading provisions and barbeque gear onto his cousin's fifty year old blue and white painted wooden boat, which had been handed down the generations in the family. Simon and Aisha walked along the harbour wall toward Panos and his family.

'Kalimera Captain!' Simon shouted.

'Ah the love birds are here. Kalimera, a beautiful day for it!' His huge voice echoed across the harbourside and a flock of gulls flew up suddenly in fright. Simon and Aisha reached the boat, and Simon set down a large crate of beer that he had brought. They hugged everyone and Simon stood back to admire Panos's attire, white cargo shorts, navy blue t-shirt, with *I'm the captain* on it, and a jaunty sailors cap, with fake gold braid, completed the look.

'You like my uniform?' enquired Panos, giving a mock salute.

'Oh yes mate, a great look, very nautical.'

'All aboard Princess Maria!' Panos boomed, and they loaded the rest of the provisions and cast off and set out for the outer harbour into calm seas. Panos had turned on the engine, as there was too little wind. He set a course for the white sea cliffs a few miles west of the capital. They could see the big mountain range of the island a few miles away, and some white dots, which were the ruins of centuries old monasteries. Most of them were ruins and tourists often remarked - that it must have been an austere and poverty stricken life.

The small blue boat left a white wave behind her as she ploughed on across the tranquil sea towards the white cliffs in the distance. A small Greek flag fluttered noisily from the stern. Most tourists never ventured this far, except on excursions, and the larger boats had too deep a draught to enter the sea caves. It was an advantage to have a small boat, which could easily navigate the shallower lagoons inside the sea caves or grottos as the locals called them. Panos slowed the engine down as they approached the caves and passed under a huge natural archway of bleached white rock and entered a magical world.

'Wow! Aisha shouted, as the little boat slowed down inside the cave, the water was the most amazing and sparkling azure blue, and the walls were covered with striated white rock formations. It was a marine amphitheatre.

'Isn't it beautiful Simon,' Panos said, as he dropped the anchor into the clearest water Simon had ever seen.

'It's incredible,' Simon replied, 'words fail me for once.'

Roula and Dimitri were the first to dive in and were soon splashing around and whooping with delight, as Elena Aisha and Simon followed them. Simon swam with strong strokes and felt the slightly chilly water flow over him. The water was so healing and cooling after the fierce heat of the sun. Aisha and Elena joined him as they trod water.

'Come on in Panos, it's so refreshing,' shouted Aisha.

'Soon,' said Panos, lighting a cigarette. 'I am working up to it gradually. And I need to be dry to light the barbeque - no.'

'You big softy,' said Simon, 'You bring us all out here and don't even get wet. 'Come in Papa,' the children shouted together.

'Ah ok if I must,' Panos replied, as he put his cigarette out on an old tin he used as an ashtray. He pulled his t-shirt off to reveal a capacious belly and made a great show of diving in, causing a huge splash as he hit the water. Everyone cheered as he surfaced, coughing and spluttering like a large sea mammal.

The little boat chugged out of the cave and over the flat- calm turquoise sea, heading for some small coves that were inaccessible from land. Panos and Eleni knew the island like the back of their hands, they'd been out here in their father's boats when they were children. They used to scramble over the rocky ledges like little mountain goats and swim in the sea like sleek baby seals. Now *their* children were doing the same - the circle continuing, endlessly down the years - generation to generation, it was the Greek way - family was everything, even now in this modern era. It was one of the things that endeared Simon to this island, that and the clear light, the sense of peace, of timelessness, of belonging. As he was the only child in his family he had missed having brothers or sisters. He knew of course that it wasn't a perfect lifestyle, although it may seem so to the tourists. It was easy for holidaymakers to project that illusion of paradise onto the locals' way of life. Panos and Eleni worked brutal hours during the season, in scorching temperatures and often surviving on very little sleep and no days off. They had their moments too, like couples the world over. His roving eye had caused tensions at times and had often pushed Eleni into giving him a proper greek woman's earbashing. Simon loved women, but he could never understand why Panos did this - when he had the most gorgeous wife. It was mostly all talk and bluster these days from Panos though - and he wasn't the only man on the island, Greek or otherwise, to fancy his chances with the young female tourists - who flocked to the island. For now though their marriage was strong - all was calm like the sea today.

'How long to go Papa, I'm hungry.' complained Roula, drying her long dark hair on a beach towel. 'Not long pedhi mou-soon be there,' her father replied, expertly guiding the boat through a shoal of jagged looking rocks.

The water became much shallower now, and Panos needed all his concentration, as he steered towards a small sandy cove a few hundred yards away.

'This is the life eh - Yamas.' Simon clinked bottles of beer with Aisha and Eleni, who were all sitting in a knot at the bow. Roula and Dimitri were on either side of the boat, their legs dangling over the side, enjoying the cooling salt spray and drinking fanta.

'It's so hot today,' said Aisha, wiping the sweat from her neck.

'Soon be time for another cooling dip,' said Eleni.'We're almost there. Eleni motioned with her hand toward the little bay they were approaching. 'We used to come here as children, Panos and I - in our fathers' boats, it holds a lot of special memories for both of us.'

'That beach looks beautiful,' said Aisha.

'A secret cove,' replied Eleni. 'No one can reach this from the land, even some locals are not aware of it, it's so hidden away.'

Panos guided the little boat expertly into the cove, as he'd done hundreds of times before. He gunned the throttle back and the engine noise died away and a puff of diesel fumes shot out the exhaust.

'Bravo Captain!' exclaimed Simon, clapping in appreciation. 'That was some feat of seamanship,'

Panos took one of his trademark theatrical bows. 'All ashore everyone - and please do not drop the barbeque in the water, like you did last year Dimitri.'

His son blushed slightly at this remark, and put on his sulky face. Panos exchanged secret smiles with his son, who was used to his father's joshing.

Panos and Simon and Dimitri did the manly thing of setting up and lighting the barbeque, and doing the cooking. The air was soon filled with heavenly scents of lamb and rosemary and oregano. Aisha helped Eleni and Roula to prepare the salad, fresh beefsteak tomatoes, cucumber, lettuce and onions, and feta and also grilled halloumi cheese and freshly made and garlicky zingy tzatziki and home-made bread.

'Mmm that smells amazing.' said Aisha.

'I take no credit Aisha, all Eleni's work, she was up late last night marinating the lamb and the kebabs. I grew the tomatoes though, oh and the potatoes, the finest on Xanthos,' he said, letting out a belly laugh. Eleni cast her eyes heavenwards - she was used to her husband's schoolboy humour.

'Here mate, get this down you.' Simon handed Panos a cool beer.

'Cheers,' replied Panos - 'Yamas everyone, to a wonderful day with fine friends and great food.'

'Yamas!' they chorused.

'This lamb is delicious, Eleni.' Simon wiped the lamb juices from his chin with a napkin.'

'Thank you,' Eleni replied. 'It's another of those old family recipes.'

'Yes amazing flavours, you must give me the recipe or is it a secret? enquired Aisha.

'No secret - I will share,' Eleni replied.

'Thanks Eleni.'

'So Simon tells us you're going back home for a while?' Eleni enquired.

'Yes, I miss my family so much.'

'Of course you do. We're so lucky here, to have all our family together, I suppose we take it for granted.'

'You have a lovely family and I love this island, but I'm sad that I haven't seen mine in a long while. I'll be back soon though. I have good reasons to.' She looked over at Simon and he smiled.

'We'll miss you at the Taverna too,' said Panos. 'You're such a hard worker and also have that lovely smile for our customers.'

'Thanks Panos, it's only for three weeks though. I'm sure you can do without me for a little while.'

'You'll enjoy seeing your family. We'll have a little celebration to welcome you back,' Eleni said.

Dimitri and Roula headed for a swim, as the adults sat on the soft sand, having a drink, and talking about this and that and how busy it was this year at the Taverna and how glad Panos and Eleni were of this small break. It was tiring work running a restaurant, and very few tourists would know the effort that went into the endless smiles and meals and drinks and late nights and long days. Why should they? They were here on holiday, to forget their own worries for a while. They too had jobs and lives back in their homelands, and they too needed a relaxing two or three weeks away - so they could escape all of that, be in a little bubble and enjoy this beautiful island.

The happy crew spent the afternoon fishing and eating and drinking and swimming and talking. The sandy little cove was an idyllic spot and the warm cerulean waters lapped at the sheltered bay, as a light breeze cooled them all down from the fierce sun.

'Thanks for a lovely day guys, it was so special to be a part of,' Simon said.

'Yes thank you both,' said Aisha, it was very special. I will always remember it.

'You are welcome my friends,' said Panos, leaning against a rock, cigarette in hand.

'Yes, it was our pleasure,' echoed Eleni. A lovely memory. 'We have an old saying here. It translates as - e*njoy the moment, as time can be a thief.*'

'That's a great saying Eleni Yes it can go far too quickly,' said Simon.

Panos sighed contentedly, then gestured over to the children, beckoning them, palm downwards in the Greek way. 'Ela! Dimitri, Roula, come and help your old Mama and Papa, to load up please.' The kids happily did as they were requested and their little paradise was reluctantly left behind, as the boat meandered its familiar way back to the harbour of Neo Horio, towards the sunset. The colours were bleeding soft pink and orange across the sky, as the heat of the day gradually began to subside. Everyone was quiet now, tired and content, as the boat chugged on. Simon looked at Aisha and he put his arm around her.

10
CATCHING UP WITH OLD FRIENDS

A few tears had been shed, before Aisha boarded the ferry to Crete. He'd waved until she was out of sight and now he felt a bit lost. They'd spent nearly every waking hour together since that night at her place. It seemed so long ago now - so much had happened. Their relationship had deepened and now they lived together. He wondered what Aisha's family would make of that. Xanthos had been a bolt hole for her, a safe haven. They'd talked about him accompanying her, but had felt that it was too soon. He didn't want to force himself upon her family. There would be time for that later. She needed to see her family and friends, but he had no such emotional family ties now, his mother and father were long gone. Oh well, he thought, *it's only three weeks. I can tidy the house and garden up a bit, do some writing and catch up with old friends I hadn't seen for some time.*

***

'Another coffee?' asked Jude.

He was sitting in their garden in the midday July sunshine.

'Can't believe it's the first time I've been back here for a while,' Simon said.

Grant was drinking his gin and tonic and reading his newspaper, chipping into the conversation now and then.

'Yes, since the Ruthven thing,' said Grant ruefully, shaking his head.

Simon felt his face flush at the mention of Ruthven.

'It's gone by so quickly and you with your new lady.' Grant continued. 'You've been a bit busy old chap, we've only met her once and that wasn't for long. Gorgeous girl though. We're sorry to hear what she's been through.'

Simon brushed his thinning hair back from his forehead and looked at the two of them. 'Yes it can be hard for her at times - all those memories. Listen, I need to say something…I want to apologise properly for that night - you know with Ruthven. It makes me cringe just thinking about….'

Jude gently interrupted. 'You *did* apologise Simon, remember you phoned the next day, which is more than the charming major did, although to be fair, Jenny called by here soon afterwards, without him knowing of course - and apologised for his boorish behaviour. That woman must be a saint to put up with him, he's a dreadful man and gives us expats a bad name. He won't be welcome back here anytime soon. I'm still in touch with Jenny though.'

Simon took a drink of his coffee. 'Yes, what he said was disgusting, but it didn't stop him pressing charges though. You probably heard I had a visit from the police - they gave me a warning. He struck a bloody raw nerve I can tell you, but I was drinking a lot at the time, and well you know - I shouldn't have let him get to me. I just wanted to make things right between you and Grant and me. I really value your friendship.'

'We feel the same, old chap,' said Grant, putting down his paper.'Look, we know you went AWOL for a while - it was understandable, but you're back with us now. Anyway, It was provocation of the highest order. Like Jude said, he's not welcome here anymore.' Grant took a large slug of his G and T.

'Now…Simon…I wasn't going to mention this…but Jude and I have discussed it…and we thought that you needed to know. Please keep what I'm about to tell you - strictly to yourself and Aisha.'

'Of course.' Simon replied.'

Grant continued. 'Jude and I befriended Donald and Jenny, when they first moved here - around 1990. We'd been living here a couple of years by then - and thought it was the right thing to do - to welcome fellow expats and all that… help them settle in. Anyway…to cut a long story short - they'd only been here a few weeks and we invited them round for dinner. Donald got extremely drunk, but he was good company back in those days, believe it or not - so different from the bitter man you see now… I remember that evening, he was regaling us with tales about his army days, amazing stuff most of it, all pretty light-hearted - and very interesting. He and Jenny had travelled the globe - been there - seen it - done it sort of thing.'

Jude came over and poured Grant another G and T from a glass jug.

'Thank you my dear… Then, as the night wore on, things became a bit more serious. He told us that he'd been posted to Northern Ireland as a young officer, and how dangerous it was - what with all the riots and the bombings. He said that one night there was a particularly bad riot...in Belfast. And that...he'd been involved in the accidental shooting of a teenage boy... He told us that he'd appeared in court to face charges and that the decision was, that it had been a terrible accident and that he'd not meant to shoot the young boy. I don't remember any more details about it - but I do remember him getting very emotional...He never mentioned it again after that night, but I've often wondered what exactly happened.'

Simon shook his head. 'That's pretty heavy stuff Grant - but nothing would surprise me about that man. A boyhood friend of mine's sixteen year old brother was shot dead in similar circumstances - during a riot in Belfast in the early '80's. I don't think the family ever got over it. I was in London at the time - and lost touch with my friend. I heard later that he'd joined the IRA, but no one could verify that of course. It's all been lost in the mists of time.'

'That's such a tragedy - those were terrible times and you did the right thing by getting out of it all.' Grant added.

Jude put down her wine glass...I remember that night with Donald Ruthven - we were a lot younger back then and we'd all had far too much to drink. My recollections can be a bit hazy - but Grant's right - that's what he told us. It's not the sort of thing you forget. Jenny's never mentioned it again either... I'm not taking sides, but it can't have been easy, being in the army over there at that time. - especially as a young soldier. They were being petrol bombed and shot at and god knows what - there were no winners that's for sure.

Simon nodded. 'That's true Jude. It was pretty hard growing up there - we were never big fans of the army, but I suppose they had their job to do - we just didn't appreciate that back then - and they didn't exactly endear themselves to the catholic population at times. I guess a lot of them were scared young men - including Ruthven... *if* I'm feeling charitable. But did he really have to carry that hatred with him all his life - and take it out on Siobhan and I, just because we were Irish? We *never* joined or supported anything to do with the IRA - that's why I finally snapped that night, enough was enough. His bullying of me and Siobhan had been going on for years... He must be a very damaged human being.'

Grant sighed and finished off his gin. 'Yes, he's a strange individual right enough.' ....Now old gal, are you going to get this man a proper drink, before he dies of thirst - and one for your old man - while you're there my darling.'

'He only calls me that when he wants a drink - or food,' Jude giggled.

Simon smiled and then went over to Jude and gave her a warm hug and shook Grant's hand.

'Thanks - true friends are hard to find.'

Jude went to get more drinks, then called back over her shoulder. 'Oh, by the way, Mags has been asking after you - she said you'd been neglecting her with your new lady.'

'Funny you should say that Jude. I'm planning to go and see the wee one. It's been ages.'

***

He spent the next week helping Panos and Eleni at the Taverna. It gave him something to do and some company whilst Aisha was away. She'd been phoning him regularly and all appeared to be well. He'd noted a calmness and softness in her voice. She sounded relaxed and was having a wonderful time with her mother and sister and brother and had been out to lunch with some of her friends.

***

Panos and Simon sat in the Taverna gardens. The fierce August sun was just setting, but it was still steaming hot. A handful of customers were enjoying a quiet beer or a cold frappe. Most of the tourists had gone back to their apartments and hotels to have a siesta before hitting the town later.

'So, she is fine, nothing to worry about. I'm glad, as she was so desperate to get home to see family and friends,' said Panos, enjoying a cigarette and a welcome break. Eleni had popped over the house to cook some dinner for the children.

'Yes mate, she seems very happy, she needed to see them and also have a break from me.' He gave a little laugh.

Panos laughed too. 'Of course she needs a break, even Eleni needs a break from *me* sometimes believe it or not.'

'Oh I believe it mate, I'd want a break from you too,' he said, reaching over and slapping Panos good naturedly on his arm.

'So, you saw Jude and Grant, now you're going to visit Mags,?' said Panos. He continued. 'I saw her in town a few weeks ago - she said that she did well this year with her singing - she made a bit of money. A real character, and such a voice for one so small.'

'Yes quite a character,' Simon agreed. 'She has the most amazing voice and she's a force of nature.'

'Please give her my best wishes when you see her.'

'Will so mate.'

Mags lived out of town, near the coastal village of Agios Nikolaos. Her centuries old traditional little house sat on a small hill overlooking a beautiful scimitar bay. A tiny monastery named after the saint was nearby and was a much visited tourist attraction. The village was once reliant on fishing, but most of the fishermen had long since sold their homes to developers for quite vast sums, to be made into holiday apartments or small hotels. It was easy money, compared to getting up at the crack of dawn in all weathers, to go out and fish. A few old boys who would go out occasionally and catch some fish for supper. Simon parked his car and walked through a small olive grove and up to the familiar old blue wooden door and knocked three times.

'Well, look what the cat dragged in.' Mags stood in her open doorway, she was nut brown, hands on hips - she wore an old gypsy hippy dress and wrists full of metal bangles, that clinked as she moved her slim expressive hands and gave Simon a lingering and warm hug. 'Where have you been hidin Irishman,' she said, in that familiar smoky drawl.

'Just ducking and diving Mags, you know me.'

Her cobalt blue eyes twinkled. 'Oh yeah I know *you* alright sonny boy, copped off with a sultry chick I hear - you know that nothin passes me by - even all the way out here.'

'I certainly do Mags.' She always made him smile - straight to the point - no messing.

'In you come then big man - great to see you - even though you've neglected me. You'll have a drink and stay over I hope. I'll cook us some dinner later.'

'That'll be great Mags. He pointed to the top pocket of his short-sleeved shirt. 'I brought my toothbrush. It's been so long. We've a lot to catch up on.'

'That we have - we surely have big man,' she replied.

They were sitting on the terrace in Mags's tiny back garden. It was full of ripening tomatoes, aubergines, onions, potatoes and pear and plum and olive trees.

'So here's to us, and who's like us,' said Mags, clinking glasses.

'Slainte - to us and good times ahead,' said Simon

So... your lady's gone back home to see her family. Poor lass - Grant and Jude told me about what she's been through - witnessing all that - must have been pure hellish.'

'Yes it was pretty harrowing for Aisha at the time - and still is. I'm surprised that she hasn't got bloody Post Traumatic Stress because of it. She's a very strong person though,' Simon replied.

'Aisha's a lovely name. One of my backing singers in the seventies had the same name. She bagged herself a lead singer with a huge rock band as I remember. His name escapes me. I'd love to meet her. Bring her over when she's back and you two love birds can stay in the bridal suite. I'll cook my lamb stifado for you.'

Simon burst out laughing. 'Bridal suite...spare- room more like. That'd be great, wee one.' He set his drink down on the mosaic table and met her gaze.

'So... what's happening with you these days Mags, anything exciting?'

Her eyes brightened as she drew heavily on a fat roll up before speaking. 'Well...funny you should ask - you'll never guess...got myself a man, a toy boy.'

'What! I mean that's feckn great - I'm so pleased for you. Where did you meet *him* then?'

Mags took a huge drag on her roll up...Max's Bar - he swaggered in one night with his ponytail and his Hawaiian shirt - a Swedish Viking - shoulders like a heavyweight boxer. I was smitten - he's a musician too, plays the guitar. He did some backing guitar with me that first night and the rest - as they say - is history. You know me Si, not easy to impress, cynical old rock chick, but he hooked me proper. I keep havin to pinch mysel.'

Simon touched her arm affectionately. 'That's amazing. I'm so happy for you. Does this Viking have a name - where does he live?'

'Sven - just down the coast at Ayia Varvara, you know the little hippy village, lives in a bloody Yurt, very new age. We see each other when we want to - share the odd spliff and you know - give each other freedom - suits me fine. - suits us both.'

'I know that village - full of new age types as you say, has a great vibe down there. I used to go there a lot with Siobhan.'

'Yeah I remember...she was such a lovely girl, I miss her.' Mags took a tissue out of her bag and dabbed her eyes.

'We all do Mags - you two were as thick as thieves...You look so happy - what age is this Viking then?

'Fifty six, seein as yer askin - and fit as a butcher's dog.'

'I *do* believe you're blushing Mags - a Swedish hippy - toy boy - guitar god - good for you, go for it - life's too short and all that.'

Mags let out a big belly laugh. 'I know... *me* at seventy with a bloody toy boy. I thought all that had passed me by. The old gals at Max's are jealous as hell - spittin feathers they are.'

Simon smiled broadly. 'I'll bet they are - never too late though - I've never seen you so happy in years Mags. This calls for a toast - where's that feckin bottle of Jamesons I brought you?'

11
WELCOME HOME

The phone rang at 6am and woke him up.

'I'm sooo sorry to ring you so early, I just needed to hear your voice.'

'It's fine darling,' he replied sleepily.' It's lovely to hear you,' as he stifled a yawn. 'Is anything wrong?'

'Everything's fine, it's been lovely to see everyone, but I want to come back - I miss you. I will come back in three days. I hope you can meet me off the ferry, it's the afternoon one.'

'I've missed you too, can't wait to see you again, see you soon darling, take care. Go back to sleep.'

'I'll try. I've missed you too, see you soon.'

On the day she was due back, he woke early and pulled on a pair of shorts and flip flops, and opened the curtains and the heavy wooden shutters, and let the early morning sunlight stream into the bedroom. He looked satisfyingly out onto the spacious gardens and heard a donkey braying mournfully somewhere in a distant olive grove. It had only been a few weeks, but he'd really missed her. Sure he had plenty of friends and he and Panos had gotten drunk a few times and had some good old chats, but it wasn't quite the same as having Aisha around. He padded downstairs and made his way into the lounge, opening more shutters as he went. The house was filled with light. He'd asked the architect to design it that way, to make the most use of it. He walked into the spacious kitchen and filled up the kettle, and switched it on and then glanced at his watch, 8am. He'd got up far too early of course, in his excitement. She wasn't due in 'til two o'clock.

He sat down at the breakfast bar and had two cups of strong coffee and some buttered toast, he could rarely face anything more substantial at that time of the morning. Then he went upstairs to shower, and enjoyed the water coursing off his body and the smell of the shower gel and felt that his senses were truly alive. He put on some sandy coloured canvas shorts, a green t-shirt, and some well worn and faded tan coloured espadrilles. He spent the rest of the morning doing some writing. He still had a contract with an Irish tourism magazine, to write an article about the island. It was a bit overdue and he needed the money, so he hastily dashed off a good few paragraphs. Around 11am he went outside, locked the front door, and started his beaten up little blue Fiat, and his first stop was Panos's to catch up, as he hadn't seen him for a while, what with all this travelling round the island and catching up with friends while Aisha was away.

It was nearly midday when he entered Pano's taverna. He walked under the vine- clad canopy and bent down - as usual, his head brushed against some bloom-covered bunches of black grapes. Panos saw him before he saw Panos.

'Kalimera stranger, we thought you had got lost. Where have you been my friend?' he called out. His familiar loud voice rang out across the tavern startling a few of his customers, and caused a couple of them to stop eating their breakfasts, and look over to see where the racket was coming from. Simon and Panos walked over to meet one another grinning and had their traditional embrace.

'Hi mate, great to see you, just been catching up with some old friends around the island, while Aisha's been away. How have you been, and how's Eleni and the family? Making plenty of money?'

'All good my friend, all good. You must tell me all about your adventures. When is Aisha due back by the way? he enquired.

'Funny you should say that, she's back today, she's coming home a bit earlier than planned. I'm picking her up off the two o'clock ferry. Any chance of a coffee and a bit of lunch mate?'

'That's great news,' said Panos,' we've missed her around here.'

'I've missed her too,' Simon winked at his friend.

'Ah of course you have - you devil. Eleni will bring your coffee.'

Simon sat down at a spare table near the bar area, while Panos went in search of Eleni. She emerged a few minutes later holding a cup of steaming coffee and had a big beaming smile. She placed the coffee on the table and Simon stood up and embraced her.

'Lovely to see you, it's been a while, We are so used to you coming here every day,' she said

'I know. I've been halfway round the island and back, catching up with some friends.'

'Well that wouldn't take long - on our tiny island. I hope they're all well.'

'All grand thanks Eleni.'

'And I hear that someone special is coming back today.' she smiled at him.

'Oh yes, Panos told you of course, he's quick off the mark. I can't wait to see her.'

'We've missed her too - and not just in the taverna. But I hope she still wants to work here though, the customers love her.'

'Just like they love you too Eleni,' he winked at her.'

'Go away you sweet talker, but thank you. It doesn't cost anything to smile.'

'Did she enjoy her visit home, her family would be so glad to see her?' she enquired.

'Yes - she said she loved seeing all her family and friends, of course,' Simon replied.

'Nw...what would you like for lunch?'

'Oh just some tuna salad please, that would be great.'

'Of course - coming up,' said Eleni brightly as she disappeared behind the bar area into the kitchen.

A little while later she appeared, carrying his food on a tray and set it before him and placed the condiments at the side, olive oil and vinegar and salt and black pepper, and his knife and fork, wrapped in the ubiquitous white napkin, seen in all tavernas and cafes throughout Greece.

'Eharisto Eleni,' said Simon

'Parakalo-Kala Orexi,' replied Eleni, as she walked back to the kitchen.

Simon was tucking into his salad when Panos appeared at his side carrying two small Mythos beers. He sat down in the chair opposite and passed one over.

'Yammas,' said Panos

'Yammas,' repeated Simon. 'To us and our loved ones.'

'Endaxi,' Panos replied, and both took a long swig of their cold beer. Simon spent the next hour having cups of coffee and chats with Panos and Eleni, when they had the time between serving people. He looked at his watch, it said 1.30pm and got up and bid farewell to his friends, before jumping in his car and heading towards the port.

It was only a ten minute journey and he arrived at the ferry port in plenty of time. He kept scanning the horizon for the big blue and white ferry. There were lots of people milling around, some waiting for the ferry, and some seeing people off. These would be mostly the locals who were visiting family on some of the nearby islands. He spotted a Greek Orthodox priest, who stood out from the crowd, with his long white beard and black stovepipe hat. There were also the usual groups of twenty something backpackers from all over Europe, heading for their next island, kissing and hugging, nut brown with the sun, and laden down with huge rucksacks and tents and sleeping mats on their backs. He spotted the ferry coming into view on the horizon, first a distant white dot, and then it grew larger as it neared the port. The crowd began to move instinctively as one huge amorphous mass towards the big barrier near the embarkation point and the ferry staff had to shout at some people who were clearly not up for queuing.

At last the big blue and white *Island Lines* ferry came nearer and he could make out the huge wash it left in its trail. It was a few hundred yards away now and he scanned the people at the guard rails to see if he could catch sight of her. The ferry staff burst into life and as the big boat came alongside with a deafening roar of its bow thrusters. The men men moved into position, ready to receive the huge ropes that were being expertly thrown their way. They quickly wrapped them around the massive harbourside bollards and secured them. Soon the ship was secured and the gangway was lifted on by a massive crane - after a few minutes the passengers started disembarking with much fanfare, laughter and shouting. He caught sight of her half way down the gangway and shouted 'Aisha!' She looked up and tried to see where his familiar was coming from and then got caught up in the throng of passengers - as they made their way into the arrivals terminal. He had to wait, while everyone went through passport control, and then she appeared - walking quickly towards him pulling her small suitcase and with a big grin on her face. They threw their arms around one another.

'I've missed you so much. How was your journey?'

'Not so bad, it just took such a long time. It's great to be back.'

He took her suitcase from her and they left the quayside holding hands and made their way to his car.

***

Simon opened the shutters and squinted in the strong early morning sun.

'What time is it?' Aisha asked sleepily.

'10.30. I need some water, Simon replied.

They had stayed up late eating and drinking and getting to know one another again.

'Can you get me some too please. Too much red vino,' she said. 'I forgot how strong Greek wine is.'

'Same here but it was worth it.'

Simon came over to the bed, kissed her forehead and handed her a glass of iced water. He gulped a few mouthfuls of his own.

'Ah that's better. What would you like to do today? Thank god Panos has given you the day off to recover from travelling.'

'A lazy day, down at the beach at Agapi would be nice, a swim and fresh fish for lunch?' she suggested.

'Sounds great,' he replied.

Agapi Ammos - or love beach in Greek, was a long, narrow bay, only twenty minutes drive from their house. YANNIS was a little taverna, famed for its seafood and it sat about a hundred yards from the beach. There was an artificial promontory made of large boulders, with the tiny church of Saint Katerina at the end. It was painted white with a blue dome and white cross on top. People prayed to the saint and left votive offerings, to ask God to cure their ills, or to listen to any emotions that were troubling them. It could be a young couple trying for a baby, or an older mother praying for a miracle cure - for her husband's cancer. It was a well used little church.

Simon and Aisha parked up and made the short trek to a quiet spot and set out their towels and bottles of water in the shelter of some rocks. They quickly stripped down to their beachwear and raced down through the burning sand - to the water and dived in.

'It's amazing - so refreshing,' gasped Aisha as she began slow breaststrokes.

'Fantastic, I've missed this,' Simon replied after spitting out a mouthful of salty brine.

They swam a few hundred yards out, then slowly made their way back towards the shore. Aisha began towelling Simon dry and he stole a kiss.

'That's nice. I've missed you, and all of this too,' she said, wrapping her arms around him. I love my family and it was so good to see them, but this place feels a million miles away from the cares of the world.'

'I feel the same, how lucky are we?' he smiled.

'Very,' she replied.

'Let's go and have some lunch shall we, I'm starving,' Simon said.

'Me too, can't wait to taste the sea bream.

They ambled up to the taverna, which was really just a wooden shack, built from various bits of old driftwood and had been extended over the years. Yannis, the owner, was the younger Yannis. His father had built the original shack in the sixties and added to it in the seventies and eighties. He was still around and sat in the back sipping ouzo most of the day, and playing Tavli with his old friends, who had shared many adventures with him over the years. Some were fishermen, with weather-beaten nut brown faces, and had many tales to tell about the old days.

Yannis junior came out to greet them - with a big smile. 'Welcome - good afternoon to you both. Yannis was a short man in his mid fifties, with a shock of thick greying hair and a protruding belly. He obviously enjoyed his wife's food. He pulled up a wickerwork chair for Aisha.

'Good afternoon and thank you Yannis,' said Aisha

'Afternoon Yannis, how are you and how's business?' Simon enquired.

'I cannot complain, my friend,' Yannis replied. Business is good, the family are well and the tourists are still here as you can see. The season seems to get longer each year. I'm not complaining though. I need the money, my youngest daughter is getting married soon - so expensive these modern weddings. I think mine and Maria's cost just a few Drachmas. He smiled 'It was so long ago I can't remember - age huh,' he said, looking upwards to the heavens in that resigned Greek way that was so familiar.

Simon smiled. 'Yes I know, everything seems to be expensive now,' he said, settling into his chair.

Yannis continued. 'Anyway - enough of my troubles, the sun is shining, the sea is calm and we're lucky to be still alive...And now, today,' he announced theatrically, 'for the special - we have fried Calamari - I caught it this morning with my spear gun out in the bay.' He gestured over his shoulder towards the gleaming expanse of sea, 'Also we have Stifado, made by Maria last night. I can recommend both. I'll leave you to relax and take your time to choose. Some drinks perhaps?

'Two small Mythos please Yannis, and a jug of water too - thank you.' Simon said.

'My pleasure.' Yannis bowed and walked slowly back into the taverna.

'What a lovely man he is, always smiling,' said Aisha.

'Yes, I remember when his father owned the place back in the day, a real character. He's in the back of the restaurant there, tippling away at his ouzo. I've had some mad nights here down the years. You wouldn't believe it if you saw him now, but Old Yannis was a fantastic Greek dancer. He did incredibly athletic jumps and turns and walked on his hands and then he'd set the floor on fire and leap over the flames - some guy. The tourists loved it. Yannis came over and set down the beers and the water, as the couple nodded their thanks.

Aisha took a sip of water, then picked up her beer. 'Can we...talk for a minute?'

'Of course - this sounds serious,' Simon replied.

'I had time to think while I was away. I know I have a nice job at the taverna and Panos and Eleni have been so good to me. I really appreciate it and don't want to sound ungrateful, but it's hardly stretching my brain and also I feel I'm not contributing enough. You pay most of the bills and I don't want to scrounge off a man, I have my pride.

'Wait a minute darling. Who says you don't pay your way? You work hard and long hours and I know the money's not brilliant, but I don't see it as... scrounging.'

'Well... whatever way you look at it, I'd rather get a better paid job and then I'd know that things were more equal, it's just the way I feel. Please try and understand.'

'I *do* understand.' Simon sounded unusually tetchy. 'I just thought things were fine the way they are. I thought you were happy.'

'I *am* happy Simon, but I also need to be an independent woman, please try and see my point of view.'

They sat in silence for a while letting things sink in. Yannis came to their table, and they ordered some food. They both looked out over the sea. Simon thought to himself: *This wasn't an argument - more a difference of opinion - they tended not to argue, but it had unsettled him. He also considered the fact that they hadn't been together that long and it had been fantastic, but also pretty intense, what with everything going on about the court case and other stuff - every relationship had its ups and downs and what Aisha was suggesting was in fact a good thing. They'd been living in each other's pockets for nearly a year now and nice though that could be, there comes a time in every relationship when the honeymoon perio*d ends *and real life intrudes.*

Simon leaned over and touched her arm.

'What sort of things are you interested in doing then?' Simon asked.

She put her hand over his. 'I have some ideas. I don't think there's a lot of call for university lecturers on Xanthos though...as we don't have a university.'

Simon laughed. 'You mentioned teaching yoga before, when I met you at your house.'

'You have a good memory. That's one of my ideas. I meant to tell you while I was away, but it didn't seem right to discuss it on the phone. I popped into the University when I was home. I spoke to my manager. They're making a lot of lecturers redundant in my department. They've offered me a good package - a lump sum and a pension. More than I would get if I retired early.' Aisha shifted in her chair and let the news sink in.

Simon took a drink of his beer and paused before replying.

'Well, that's good news - isn't it? You were saying that you'd had enough of lecturing a while back.'

'Yes, and my sabbatical comes to an end in January and I'll be fifty in two years' time. Maybe I need a different direction?'

'Fifty's not old - what do you think you want to do?'
'I know it's not - but I need a change. Maybe we can leave it for a while and chat more about it another time.' She sounded irritated.

'Maybe.' he finished his beer and got up to leave.

12

A NIGHT AT MAX'S BAR

Max's Bar was legendary on Xanthos. It was on the main strip overlooking the harbour and cheesy as hell, but very popular with expats and tourists. Simon bent down under the narrow old doorway as he entered, holding Aisha's hand. "Yes Sir I can Boogie" boomed out from the speakers. The place was *stowed out* as they would say in Ireland.

'Jesus it's busy,' Simon said, as he scanned the room trying to find a spare table.

'This isn't busy, you need to get out more old man,' Aisha replied, pushing him playfully in the small of the back. 'I can't believe I'm meeting *thee* Mags Morrison. I told you, one of my tutors at University had all her albums, and he used to play her records in our classes. We all grew to love her.'

'You'll love her in the flesh too - she's pretty direct, mind you. It's been a while since I was out on a Saturday night,' Simon said, 'a long while actually.' He could hardly hear his own voice amid the throng. Then he caught sight of a familiar face. 'There she is... Mags!' he shouted.

Mags recognised Simon and she beckoned him over. He and Aisha fought through to the end of the bar and Mags stood up from the table she was sitting at - and gave Simon a huge bear hug.

'How's it goin big man?' she asked, in her half Scottish - transatlantic drawl and without waiting for an answer - she continued. 'This must be the lady that the whole island's been talkin about.'

'This is Mags - Mags meet Aisha.'

'How are you, Aisha - lovely to meet you at last darlin.' She gave Aisha a huge hug and kissed her on both cheeks.'

'Hi Mags, I've heard *so* much about you from Simon, so glad to finally meet you.'

'Damn pretty too McCardle, look after her won't you,' Mags said.

'I will Mags - don't worry,' Simon said.

'Oh... How could I forget... this is Sven. I told you about him when I saw you a while back Simon,' she said, gesturing over to a very tall, stocky, blond pony-tailed man, sitting on his own. He stood up and came over to the group, smiling. He must have towered a good five or six inches above Simon, who was no short arse himself.

Simon extended his hand. 'Nice to meet you Sven,' This is Aisha. Simon felt his hand being crushed by the man's vice-like grip.

'Likewise Simon, good to meet you,' Sven replied in his deep Swedish tones, as he nodded to Aisha and shook her hand more carefully this time.'You too Aisha.'

'Come over and sit with us big man,' Mags said. 'We must celebrate.'

Simon ordered some drinks and they managed to squeeze into a small table. Mags fiddled with the many bracelets on her left arm, and took a slug of her Gin, before fixing her gaze on Simon.

'So, how are things with you now Irish man? They look pretty good from here'

'Doing fine thanks Mags, everything's grand with the world, still writing a bit - you know, surviving.'

'That's great, and you my darlin, how do you put up with this mad Irish fella?'

Aisha let out a laugh. 'He's not so bad, you know - if I keep him under control.'

'He said you might be settling here and maybe making it your home, is that right?' This was the legendary directness that Aisha had been warned about by Simon.

'We shall see, a lot to think about.'

'Good for you darlin, keep him on his toes eh.'

Sven had been sitting quietly through all of this. Simon leaned forward in his chair towards Sven and raised his voice - to be heard over the clamour.'

'Mags tells me you're a therapist, is that a new age thing? Forgive my ignorance.'

'I do bodywork,' he replied. 'It's a bit like physiotherapy- but more, you know, spiritual if you like. I have a small practice in Agia Varvara, not far down the coast from Mags. It doesn't pay that much, but I survive and I'm happy,' he said looking over at Mags and smiling.

'That sounds great Sven, and Mags said you live in a yurt?' Simon continued.

Sven smiled. 'Well... it's part of our lifestyle, you know the spiritual thing. It seems to work. It's not ideal in the Summer heat, but it's a good image for my business. I also have a small cottage nearby, which I live in most of the year. There's quite a few of us in our little community, writers, artists and creative types, I guess you'd call us - without sounding too pretentious - we're surprisingly normal once you get to know us, eh Mags?'

'Almost normal babes,' Mags said, smiling.

'Still singing?' Simon asked.

'Just about to go up, - open mic tonight.'

'That's great, haven't heard you for ages.'

As if on cue, Sven raised his vast bulk from the table and led Mags gently by the hand and through the heaving Saturday night throng. People parted willingly as the couple strode towards the little stage in the corner. Sven bent down to give Mags a kiss.

'Good luck girl,' he whispered in her ear and returned to the table.

Mags spoke a few words to Johny, the lead guitarist, who she'd known for years. He nodded a few times and spoke to the bass player and drummer. 'Southern Nights,' were an all British band and had been playing at Max's for as long as anyone could remember.

Johny came to the mic. '*Good Evening Everyone!* I hope you enjoyed that last number on this lovely Saturday night. We love playing here, with such a tasteful and appreciative crowd.'

This was followed by some raucous whistling and good - natured ribald comments.

'*Get on with it!* someone shouted from the back.

Mags stood patiently by Johny's side, smiling - she'd heard it all before.

'Ok Ok - calm down - here goes. *Tonight*! I have the great pleasure of introducing... a legend at Max's...and a legend in rock music. We're very privileged to have with us ... all the way from Glasgow, by way of New York, London and Paris...the pocket rocket, the tiny terror, that is...*Mags Morrison*! *Take it away Mags! Two three four!*

Mags nodded to the crowd and grabbed the mic, and the little five feet two middle - aged woman, miraculously transformed herself into the rock star she once was. She waited for the opening beat and joined in, perfectly on time.

'*You took me by the hand... and r e s c u e d me from l o n e l i n e s s!*'
It was the well known intro to one of her many famous songs. The crowd went wild.

'Didn't you didn't yooooo!'

Her rasping, whisky soaked voice had lost a bit of its power, but she could still hit most of the high notes and her timing was perfect, as she stood stock still and sang directly into the microphone as she'd always done back then. '*Didn't you, didn't you r e s c u e me!*'

Simon and Aisha were transfixed. Simon had seen Mags perform many times before, but having Aisha with him, made it even more special.

'Not bad eh?' Simon shouted in Aisha's ear.

'Unbelievable! Fantastic!' she shouted back. 'What a voice!'

Mags finished her set to rapturous applause and took a huge theatrical bow.

'Thanks everyone, thanks so much!'

'More More!' the crowd shouted - the noise was at fever pitch.

Johny took back the mic. 'Thank you Mags... that was f a n t a s t i c - as ever. Mags will be singing some more a bit later, don't worry. *Mags Morrison* folks,' he said, signing off. The band left the stage - to take a well earned break.

Sven and Mags fought through the crush and sat down. Mag took a large swig of her whisky.

'That was fantastic Mags, what a performance. Haven't heard you for ages, I love that song.' Simon said.

'Cheers big man, I love singin it, as long as everyone else enjoys it.'

'That was amazing, what a voice you have,' Aisha said.

'Thanks darlin, still got it eh? You'd be a bit young to remember me I guess, but as long as you enjoyed it.'

'Of course I remember you - my tutor at University had all your albums, and introduced us students to you. I never dreamed I'd meet you face to face.'

'Tutor eh, what age was he then, a hundred and five?'

Aisha burst out laughing. 'You're funny Mags - you make me smile,' said Aisha

Mags took a large slug of her whisky. 'Never take myself too seriously darlin, eh Simon.'

'Absolutely Mags, life's far too short for all that shenanigans.'

'Seen anything of Grant and Jude?' Simon asked.

'Saw them a few weeks ago - they're doin ok. Jude's sold lots of her stuff this Summer, to the tourists - so talented that gal.'

'Yes, her pottery's really original,' Simon said, and turned to Aisha. 'You must meet them - a lovely couple.'

'I'll look forward to that,' said Aisha.

Sven's met them, got on like a house on fire with Grant,' said Mags.

'Grant's a real old school character,' said Sven.

Mags had performed another number - and this had also gone down a storm. It was nearly closing time and people were starting to drift off. The little group made their way onto the pavement outside, after Mags had said her protracted goodbyes to the band. This involved much air kissing and lots of bear hugs.

'Night Mags!' shouted Johny as they were leaving. 'Take care my little darling.'

Mags lit up a cigarette as soon as she was outside and sat at one of the metal tables overlooking the harbour. The yacht's masts were clanking in the darkness and the sea was gently lapping against the harbour wall. A gentle breeze ruffled the palm trees lining the front.

'It's been great to see you both. We must do it again soon, before Winter sets in,' Simon said.

I'd love that,' Aisha added.

'Me too,' said Sven.

'That'd be a great big man, 'Mags replied. 'It was lovely to meet you at last, Aisha. Night darlins - take care you two.'

After copious hugs all round Simon and Aisha headed for the nearby taxi rank, their goodbyes echoing into the still night.

13

SMOKE SIGNALS

A few weeks later Simon and Aisha were walking along the harbourside, when they spotted a plume of smoke coming from the Ayia Varvara area, close to where Sven lived, down the west coast. People on the quayside were gathering in little knots and stopping to look at it. Some were pointing up at the sky and shaking their heads. Simon and Aisha stopped too.

'That doesn't look good,' Simon said.

'No, not good at all,' replied Aisha

'Simon, Simon!' someone shouted his name as they stood looking up at the drifting smoke.

Simon looked round and saw Grant and Jude walking quickly towards them.

'I'm too ruddy old for this,' said Grant, as he reached them, looking extremely red in the face and puffing heavily. Jude arrived just behind him and they both took a minute to catch their breath.

'Hi, what's going on?' Simon pointed up at the sky and the smoke plume, which seemed to be getting thicker and larger. 'Sorry, forgive my manners, this is Aisha.'

Grant extended his hand. 'Nice to meet you my dear.'

Aisha shook his hand. 'Lovely to meet you both,' she said, reaching over to shake Jude's hand.

'What's going on mate?' Simon asked again. 'We don't usually have forest fires at this time of year?'

Grant explained. 'They reckon it's either arson or some damn fool dropping a cigarette. Mags phoned us earlier, her boyfriend Sven lives in the area - she's worried sick. He's been told to leave. She said he's very stubborn though and wants to stay and protect his property. Most people have left already apparently.'

'We only saw them a few weeks ago, she probably told you it was the first time we'd met Sven, he seemed like a good bloke,' said Simon.

'Yes, Mags told us you'd met him, such a damn shame, I hope he and his friends are ok, some of them live in flimsy bamboo structures on the beach apparently. They'll go up like tinder if the fire reaches their village. We don't have the biggest fire service, as you know and these fires are difficult to contain - because of the steep hills. Mags said that they're thinking of bringing in those big water planes from Crete - to help put out the fires.'

Simon sighed. 'Bloody hell, that's a bastard for those poor people and all their olive groves, thank God they've just finished the harvest.'

'Yes,' said Jude sympathetically. 'Just when they should be relaxing after the season, putting their feet up - this happens.'

'This is so sad, said Aisha. 'It's people's homes and livelihoods.'

'I'll phone Panos, he'll know what's going on,' Simon said, in a decisive tone.

'That's a good idea old man,' said Grant. 'He'll definitely know what's happening.'

Simon shook his head. 'Oh well, let's hope they manage to get them under control - do you want to join us for a coffee, it's been far too long.'

'We'd love to,' Grant replied.

They made their way along the harbour - it had quietened down as it was off - season, most of the pleasure craft and tourist boats were moored up for the Winter and many of the tourist cafes had closed. They found a table at Marios, which was frequented by the locals.

Mario walked over to their table. 'Good Morning, welcome...some fire huh,' he said, gesturing to the sky.

'Yes, quite a worry Mario,' answered Grant, as they all sat down at a table overlooking the harbour.

Everyone was looking up at the sky - no one could take their eyes off it.

Jude frowned. 'I do hope everyone's going to be ok.' 'The local news said they'd evacuated everyone from the coastal villages near the fire, just to be on the safe side.'

'Yes, apart from stubborn buggers like Sven eh,' said Simon.

'You only met him once, don't be so hard on him. He just wants to protect his property,' Aisha reprimanded him.

'Yes I know darling, but how's he going to save his property when there's a raging fire around him?'

Jude sighed. 'I remember one year, not long after we moved here in '96 - when something similar happened and it reached the coast near Minos. Luckily they had managed to evacuate it in plenty of...'

Simon cut in. 'That's my point Jude, *they* listened to advice. Sven's obviously going to be the last man standing by the sounds of it. Don't get me wrong, I've only met him once, and he seemed a great bloke, but why risk your life over a bloody house. You can always build another one.'

Aisha hit right back. 'Yes and if it was *your* house, the house in the olive grove, I'll bet you'd be the last man standing too Simon McCardle, so don't go all holier than thou on us, it doesn't suit you.'

Simon smiled sheepishly. 'Yeah I know, you're probably right.'

'I *know* I'm right,' said Aisha smiling.

Grant cleared his throat. 'Aisha's right, we know you only too well, you're just as headstrong as Sven and believe me he *is* a great guy, and Mags is totally crazy about him. He's made her happy.

'Can anyone else taste the smoke?' Jude asked?' 'It's acrid - horrible. The wind won't help.'

'Yes *I* can.' said Aisha. It's filling the air. Let's hope they get it under control soon.'

Simon felt his phone vibrate in his pocket and took it out. 'It's Mags, better take it, excuse me. Hi Mags, what's up?' The other three looked carefully at Simon. 'I see, yes, funny enough, I'm with Grant and Jude right now - at Marios, they've explained about Sven. But surely if he's not listening to *you* and his friends - he's hardly going to listen to *me* - a total stranger ....Jesus, I've only met him once Mags. Ok... I'll give it a go, but they've probably blocked off the roads by now - the only way in will be by sea. I'll speak to Panos and we'll see if we can use his cousin's boat. I'm not a miracle worker though - but I'll do my best. I'll be in touch. Try not to worry too much...bye..'

Simon put the phone back in his pocket. 'I think you heard enough of my side of the conversation. Mags wants me to go and persuade Sven to leave his village.'

'Just try your best Simon darling,' Jude said, putting her hand on his arm.

'Yes, just do your best, old man,'Grant added. 'I'd come with you - but I'm a bit past all these adventures now.'

'I'll come with you,' said Aisha.

'No, No, it's too dangerous.'

'I'm not a fragile wallflower. I'm from Bosnia, remember,...we went through a war.'

'Ok you win. I have to phone Panos, excuse me.'

14

FOREST FIRES

Panos met Simon and Aisha down at the Marina. His cousin Stavros was carrying fuel on board the boat, in a big metal jerry can.

Panos was standing by the gangway looking impatient. 'Come!' he shouted. 'We have no time, I just heard the fires are reaching the west coast.'

'Ok mate, let's get going,' Simon said and he and Panos and Aisha leapt aboard. Panos cast off, just as his cousin jumped off the boat.

'Look after her for me cousin.'

'Will do Stav. Thanks for lending her to me.' Panos waved, as he steered the boat away from the quayside.

'I really appreciate this mate,' said Simon as he joined Panos in the wheelhouse.

'No problem. I just can't understand why this crazy Swedish guy wants to risk his life for a house.' Panos stroked his beard.

'I agree mate, but I promised Mags I'd try and talk sense into him - I'll tell you one thing though I won't be fighting him - he's fucking huge.'

'You're a typical alpha male - we won't have to fight him, we can talk him round,' Aisha said.

Panos steered the small boat expertly out of the harbour and into open sea. Its vibrantly painted green and red hull stood out against the emerald water, as it cut through the waves, throwing up spray onto the forward deck. A tattered little blue and white Greek flag flapped from the stern, as the boat ploughed on. The large stylised eyes painted in blue and white, to ward off the evil eye, were emblazoned on both sides of the bow, as was the custom in Greece.

Their journey took just over an hour. As they rounded the top of Cape Drapanon in the north west, they could see the full extent of it. The fire was burning through the cypress trees and olive groves on the hillside above Ayia Varvara and was clearly spreading down the hills towards the other coastal villages. A fire department helicopter was flying overhead making a terrible racket and they could see teams of firefighters in green high vis gear, up in the olive groves, beating the flames out and digging fire breaks. Everyone on board felt the radiated heat and heard the crackling and explosions of burning wood in the olive groves, as they approached the narrow harbour entrance. The smoke was much denser now and Aisha started coughing and covered her face with a scarf.

'I'd like to catch the bastards who started this,' Panos said. 'What fools, putting people's lives at risk... *Malakas*!' Panos spat out the colourful Greek word for wanker.

They're not sure if it's arson or not mate - but if it is I hope they catch the eejits soon,' Simon replied.

Simon walked to the stern and sat beside Aisha - she was gazing out to the rocks below some massive sea cliffs. He put his arm around her waist. 'He's a bit wound about the aresholes who started these fires.'

'I don't blame him - he was born and bred here,' replied Aisha.

'And he lost a good friend in a similar fire a few years ago - so that accounts for his anger - he doesn't talk about it... I've not been around this side of the island much, it has a wild beauty.'

'It's amazing, such a pity we had to see it in these circumstances,' said Aisha.

'Not many people come round here, a bit remote I suppose, some fishermen perhaps. There's some beautiful beaches, as you see and if you want to get away from people for a while and get some peace and quiet, then this is your place,' Simon said.

Panos turned around to face them, his face looked unusually serious. 'Ok my friends, we're nearing the harbour, I must concentrate now, there are many rocks here and I need to be careful.' Panos was fully focused on his task, as he guided the little boat through the rocky shallows and to the mouth of the old harbour.

Ayia Varvara was a scenic little coastal village with a few hundred inhabitants, mainly the so-called *alternative* community of New Age travellers and artists. They lived peacefully, side by side with the older island residents and made a living selling their artwork, such as driftwood sculptures and also provided various therapies. Aisha noted the quirky hippy yurts and beach shacks - as the boat came closer to the quay. They could just make out through the smoke, the pretty little white crossed church up on the hill above the village, in memory of the saint. The fires looked dangerously close to it. There weren't any people about, only a few stray - scrawny cats, nosing around the beach for something to eat.

Panos brought the boat into the quay and throttled the engine back. He noticed a very tall, scruffy, thin young man in his thirties, sitting on a bollard smoking and the man jumped up to help as they docked. Panos threw the ropes to him and the three crew jumped on to the quayside. The tall man tied the ropes around a bollard. Simon walked up to him and put his hand out to greet him.

'Morning. Thanks for that. I'm Simon. Mags's friend. We're here to see Sven. We're in a hurry. Can you show us where he lives.'

'I'm Alfred, nice to meet you,' he said, shaking Simon's hand.

'Come to talk him into leaving eh?' Alfred had a soft German accent. 'Mags has been trying to persuade us for days. There's only the two of us left, we're determined not to leave - it's taken us so long to build all this. His hand swept along the scene behind him. We're stuck here now. The road out of the village is completely cut off, we heard.'

'Look we're wasting time - we must go and find Sven,' Aisha interrupted, with some urgency in her voice. 'Please take us to him.'

'Of course - follow me - it's not far,' Alfred replied.

The little group walked quickly through the abandoned village and they could see that the fires were starting to spread down the hill and black ash was falling and sticking to their clothes. They found it difficult to breathe properly. The firefighters and Sven and Alfred had worked most of the night to dig out firebreaks on the outskirts of the village. The choking smoke was now hanging in the air as they walked and they all started coughing violently as they got nearer Sven's yurt.

Alfred stopped at the entrance to the large wickerwork structure and shouted inside. 'Sven you have visitors.'

There was a pause, then Sven emerged. His huge bulk filled the entrance and his face and shovel-like hands were soot blackened and his blonde hair was matted and filthy. Panos took a step backwards as Sven emerged, startled by the size of him.

He ran his hands through his filthy hair and smiled. 'We meet again. Mags warned me you'd be coming, but I'm afraid you're wasting your time - I'm staying put here and so is my friend.' He looked over at Alfred, who put both his thumbs up in an *Ok* gesture.

Simon stepped forward. 'This is my friend Panos, you know Aisha, we borrowed Panos's cousin's boat to come over here.'

Panos nodded.

'I've been to your taverna, great Stifado,' said Sven

'Thank you my friend.' Panos bowed.

Simon continued. 'Look Sven, we've only just known you a few weeks and maybe you think we have a cheek coming here trying to persuade a grown man to come back with us. But it's Mags you see. Panos and I have known her for many years and she clearly thinks the world of you. We agreed to come over and try and persuade you to come back with us. How do you and Alfred think you can stop the flames if they reach here? They may not of course but is it worth taking the chance?

Sven sighed. 'We've been working through the night with the firefighters, digging fire breaks. We're quite confident we can contain it even if it does reach the village. I'd like to thank you all though for thinking of me and for making that journey. I don't want to sound ungrateful - but I need to protect my property.'

Aisha noticed that Simon was casting nervous glances up towards the burning hillside. She stepped forward and used her university lecturer's tone of voice. 'Look Sven - Mags is very worried about you. It's clear that you're your own man, and it would obviously be futile trying to talk you out of it. How would you feel if we spent the day with you here, digging the firebreaks. Would that be helpful?'

Panos looked quickly at Simon with a frown. Simon was thinking - *what's she fucking doing? We're supposed to be persuading him to get away from danger.*

'What do you say guys, would that be helpful?' Aisha said.

'It's not what we were expecting, but it's very welcome, thank you all - I'll phone Mags. I'm sure it won't be the news she's been hoping for. She wants me out of here,' Sven replied.

'One step at a time I guess,' said Simon.

'You can all stay tonight in my cottage,' he said, pointing towards a small whitewashed building down the track.

'I'll sleep here in the yurt But first we must get out of this bloody smoke and have FIKA.'

'FIKA, what's that?' asked Simon.

'It's a break, time out - a tea break - or should I say a coffee break in Sweden. Am I right Sven?' asked Aisha.

'I'm very impressed,' the big man replied.

'Ok please follow me,' Sven said quickly. 'I'll sort out some food and bedding later. He led them down a path about a hundred yards through an olive grove, to his cottage, which looked like it had been there a very long time. There were two tiny bedrooms and Sven divided the rooms up between everyone. Simon noticed Panos's expression. He had never seen him looking so nervous or serious.

'I must phone Eleni - she'll be worried, this is the first night we'll have ever spent apart in twenty five years of marriage.' said Panos.

'It'll do her good, mate - give her a break from you, give her ears a rest,' said Simon.

After their coffee, Sven dished out some mattocks, spades and pickaxes, and showed them where he wanted the fire breaks dug out. He and Alfred had obviously been busy these last few days and had dug out some quite impressive trenches. He pointed up to the blazing fires on the hillside. There were crackling sounds coming from the olive groves as the fires took hold. The smoke was much denser here.

Simon felt the ash land on his shirt and brushed it off. He thought to himself - *if things don't improve by the morning we're out of here- Sven can do what he feckin wants.* He wasn't about to become a martyr. Sven had given them all some old scarves and they wore them as smoke masks. They quickly got to work on the fire breaks, and everyone kept a slightly nervous eye on the progress of the fire on the hillside. The thick, swirling smoke continued on its path. Simon felt the sweat trickling down his back and his clothes reeked.

They heard the sound of a vehicle approaching and everyone looked around. A large Xanthos Fire Service truck barrelled down the road towards them, kicking up dust and pebbles.

'I thought the road was closed off Sven,' Simon said.

'So did I,' Sven said, looking puzzled.

The truck drew level with Sven and a short burly man got out, wearing a high viz jacket, with some words in Greek that Simon translated as *'Fire Chief.'* He had a soot blackened face and hands. Sven had met him a few days before.

'Good morning. I see that you are still here and you have company,' said the Fire Chief, gesturing at everyone. 'They weren't here the other day when I visited. He spotted Panos. For the love of God what are you doing here? Panos and the Fire Chief had gone to primary school together.

Panos looked sheepish. 'Hi Dimitri - just helping friends out - with the fire breaks. We sailed over this morning. We're trying to persuade them to leave - for their own safety, but it looks like it's not working.'

'I see, good luck with that then - I've been trying for days. This is foolish

Panos - it's no use staying here, this is a dangerous area. What does Eleni think of all this mad adventure?'

'She doesn't know we're staying the night yet - she's expecting me back this evening.'

He shook his head. 'You're like a bunch of schoolkids. I thought *You* would have more sense Panos.' He came closer to Sven. 'Mr Olaffson. I am giving you another twenty four hours and then you *must* leave - all of you - or you'll be arrested. I hope I make myself clear... And just for your information, the wind is forecast to strengthen later, some high gusts are expected, so it's going to spread quickly in some places. Please be careful. I will be calling back tomorrow - and that's a promise.'

Sven nodded. 'Yes I understand Chief.'

'Twenty four hours.' The Chief pointed at this watch, and jumped in his truck. He drove off up the hill kicking up swirling clouds of dust.

Sven sighed. 'Ok folks - well I guess you can't say it clearer than that. We'll dig a few more fire breaks then call it a day and see what the morning brings. You all must be starving. Do you want to give us a hand with dinner Panos - seeing as you're the taverna man?'

Panos's face opened up into a broad smile. He looked relieved to be getting a break.

'My pleasure,' Panos replied cheerily.

'Now let's get the hell out of this damn smoke - before we all choke to death,' Sven said.

He led them back to his cottage and they sat down on wooden stools in the kitchen. 'There's a shower in the bathroom and clean clothes in the drawers in the bedrooms. They may be a little large for you guys. Aisha, Mags has left some clothes in the wardrobe - they should do the job for now.'

'Thanks Sven,' Aisha said

'Panos. I'll show you where everything is in here to make supper.'

'Great - I'm looking forward to it,' Panos replied.

Sven looked over at Simon. 'Can you give me a hand to shift something outside please my friend. We'll be back shortly,' Sven explained.

Sven and Simon walked into the garden and Sven pointed to the burning hillside. 'It's getting worse, as you see. I didn't want to say it in front of the others... but up there - where the blackened area is, it's spread a lot since yesterday.'

'So... what's the plan?' Simon replied.

'We stay the night and re-assess in the morning. I know you are all going back tomorrow. I didn't expect you to stay as long as you have. I've put your lives at risk and I don't feel good about it.'

Simon placed his hand on Sven's shoulder. 'Mate you're a great guy, I can tell that even by the short time I've known you, but you're as stubborn as a fucking mule. Look up there,' he said, pointing upwards to the scorched hills. 'It's getting closer - and the Chief told you about the winds coming later. I know you think you're a Viking - but do you really think you have some miraculous fucking Nordic powers to tame this fire? And by the way, no fucker's going to get a wink of sleep here tonight. We're off in the morning mate, and if you and Alfred have any sense left you'll join us.'

Sven sat down on an upturned wheelbarrow and shook his head back and forth. 'You are right to be angry Simon. I'm a stubborn bastard, but that's the way I am. I'm just me.'

'I'm kind of similar mate - the Celts and Scandinavians have much in common - for example, being stubborn bastards - but enough's enough.'

Sven smiled, then stood up - and came over and offered his hand to Simon. 'You win - we'll take that lift on the boat in the morning - if the invite's still open?'

'Of course it is,' said Simon, shaking his hand.

'Come - we must eat,' urged Sven.

Panos and Eleni were busy preparing food in the kitchen when they came back.

'Where's Alfred?' Sven asked.

'Gone to his own place for a shower,' said Aisha. 'He said he'll be over for dinner later.

'Well I can see that I'm not needed here,' said Sven.

'Simon - you use the shower first, I'm going outside for a cigarette.'

'Not enough smoke already in the air for you then Sven,' Aisha said smiling.

Sven dished out some beers from the fridge, and Simon quickly sank his down, to wash the soot out of his throat. The rabbit stew Panos and Aisha had prepared was wolfed down by everyone - after the hard physical labour of the day.

Panos kept holding his back and wincing in pain. 'I'm not cut out for this mate. I haven't done any proper exercise for years.'

'You'll be fine, you'll soon be back in the taverna knocking back the Ouzo - that'll take the pain away,' Aisha said.

'I bloody hope so,' Panos replied.

'I have some Ouzo. I'll find it for you Panos,' Sven said. Then he slowly stood up and addressed them all.

'Ok... I have something to say...Simon and I have been discussing things and I have decided that enough is enough. We're going back with you on the boat tomorrow, if your very kind offer is still open. I'll speak to Alfred when he comes back. I hope he'll agree.'

Aisha put her drink down. 'That's a relief, thank God Sven, we can all see that the fire's spreading. You've made the right decision. Have you told Mags?.

'Just texted her. She's very pleased,' said Sven.

'Pleased, that's an understatement surely?' Aisha said.

Sven continued. 'Simon and I are staying up to cover the fire watch tonight, we can't take any chances. The rest of you are very welcome to help out too, but only if you want to. Simon's doing the first four hours.' Sven looked at his watch. 'It's nearly midnight now, so I'll take over at 4am. I know it's not going to be easy to get sleep, but try and rest...oh and I would keep your outdoors clothes handy beside you- we may have to leave in a hurry. Panos, if everything goes ok tonight can we leave at first light please my friend, that's about 7am, is that ok?'

'Yes of course - we should be back in Neo Chorio by 8am if all goes well.'

'I'll keep you company Simon,' said Aisha. 'I won't sleep anyway.'

'Thanks darling.'

'Ok everyone, let's try and get some sleep, I know it won't be easy. Simon - I'm sleeping in the Yurt. Please do not hesitate to wake me, if you have the slightest concerns.'

'Will do, mate.'

Night fell. Simon and Aisha sat outside the kitchen scanning the fires. A few bats flitted in and out the olive grove. The fires illuminated the skyline and the thick smoke was ever present in the air. Both of them had scarves around their mouths and noses.

'We should probably move inside - this smoke's horrible, and we can see just as well from the kitchen window,' Simon said.

'Yes it's choking me - maybe we should have left earlier

'Think we missed that opportunity and besides, Panos hates sailing in the dark - he likes to see where he's going.'

The two of them slipped quietly inside the kitchen trying not to make too much noise. They could hear Panos snoring gently in the next room. Aisha flicked the kettle switch on, then took her scarf off her face. Simon did the same.

'That's better, I can breathe now,' she said, with some relief in her voice... 'I was surprised when Sven decided to come back with us tomorrow. What did you say to persuade him?'

'Just pointed out he was a mad fucker - putting himself and everyone else at risk, nothing fancy - straight talking. And besides, it was *you* who went off script and chucked in the suggestion that we stay and help them, instead of persuading them to leave with us immediately - as we'd agreed by the way, madam.'

'I just thought it was going to be futile - trying to argue with a man like Sven.'

'So...you adopted the feminine wiles routine - well it seemed to work.

She smiled. 'There are many ways to persuade people - sometimes you have to try a different approach.'

'Well whatever it was it worked. Here's to our combined negotiating skills,' said Simon and they clinked their mugs of tea together.

It was approaching 1am. Both of them had dozed off through sheer exhaustion.

***

It was 6.30am. A loud crack punctured the air and Simon was the first to waken.

'*What the fuck*! Aisha wake up - wake up!' he shouted, shaking her shoulders - 'It's the fire - it's reached us -it's here!'

He rushed out into the night air and could immediately feel the heat from the fire. He noticed large flames illuminating the olive grove about three hundred yards away - the wood crackled and snapped in the heat.

'*Fucksake*!' he shouted. 'It's nearly here, quick, wake Panos, I'll wake Sven and Alfred.'

Aisha started shouting 'Fire Fire! and ran towards Panos's room, 'Wake up Panos- wake up.'

Simon was sprinting towards Sven's yurt, his lungs were burning from the hot smoke. 'Sven Sven *Fire Fire!* wake up.' Sven's vast bulk was already emerging from the entrance and he was pulling his trousers up quickly. Alfred appeared suddenly out of the smoke. 'Alfred we must leave, now! Simon shouted.

'It's here Sven - hurry the fuck up, we must get away!' Simon said.

'Ok Ok - I'm coming man.'

Simon ran back to the cottage. Panos was up and nearly dressed.

'Mother of god - what's going on?' said Panos, his eyes filled with fear.

'Fire's spread mate - it's at the bottom of the garden, it must have jumped the fire break. Hurry man - we've got to get to the boat. You got the key?'

'Of course,' Panos said, holding up the key.

The fire was getting closer now, it illuminated the whole garden area and they could feel the intense radiated heat and see the flames licking the olive trees. The wood crackled fiercely as it moved and the smoke became thicker. Simon could hear the firefighters shouting on the hill above them. It had obviously taken them by surprise too.

Sven appeared in the doorway. Alfred was with him.

'We go... now!' shouted Sven. 'Quickly.'

Simon took a hold of Panos by the shoulder, and pushed him forward and they all started running down toward the marina. Sven led the way, with Alfred just behind him, then Aisha and Simon and Panos. Simon was virtually dragging Panoos by his shirt sleeve. Panos slowed down - then stopped completely, he was clearly struggling and he was bent over double - with his hands on his thighs and taking huge deep breaths.

'Please Simon - stop, I can't breathe...I beg you.'

'No Panos - keep going - hurry hurry!' Simon grabbed his t-shirt and pulled Panos upright and started running again, dragging him onwards in the darkness

'We're nearly there mate. I'll sort the ropes out you get us off this fucking beach.'

They all arrived at the quayside and bent over momentarily - to catch their breath. Simon looked back quickly, the fire was now near the kitchen door of Sven's cottage - another few minutes and they would have been roasted alive or died from smoke inhalation.

'Right everyone get onboard, no time to lose!' Simon shouted.

'Sven, you grab the forward ropes.' Simon undid the ropes from the after bollard and by this time Panos was inside the cabin, followed by Asha and Alfred.

Panos took the ignition key from his pocket - his hands were shaking- and he dropped the key.

He quickly picked it up and put it in the ignition and turned it over. The engine coughed a couple of times and it looked like it wasn't going to start. Aisha and Alfred shot worried glances at one another. It took several attempts to start the engine, then suddenly it roared into life and Aisha could see the fear and panic disappear from Panos's eyes.

'Thank the Lord,' Panos said, smiling broadly.

Aisha put her hand on his shoulder reassuringly. 'It's ok Panos, you're doing great, we're all with you.'

Simon and Sven were pushing the boat away from the quayside with boat hooks.

Alfred helped pull Sven on board and Simon jumped onboard after him. 'Ok mate we're good to go!' Simon shouted to Panos. His voice was croaky from the smoke and panic.

Panos opened up the throttle and the engine roared as the boat quickly gained speed out of the harbour. Aisha and Alfred nearly fell over as it accelerated.

'Slow down a bit mate, the rocks are up ahead,' shouted Simon.

'Ok, sorry everyone.' Panos fumbled in his pocket and pulled out his cigarettes, and put one in his mouth with some difficulty. His hands were shaking as he tried to light it. Aisha took his lighter from him and lit his cigarette. He took a long drag and exhaled and he looked calmer - as he lowered his speed in order to negotiate the rocks at the harbour entrance, which wasn't easy. It wasn't quite light yet and the visibility was made worse by drifting smoke from the shore.

Panos stopped just outside the harbour entrance, as the first pink, misty light of dawn shimmered above the glassy sea. The others gathered at the stern and watched in horrified fascination at the conflagration in the distance. Sven and Alfred stood together in silence, as the fire took hold of Sven's little cottage - devouring everything in its path like a wild animal. It consumed his beloved yurt that he'd spent many months building. Alfred's little shack was close by, built from offcuts of timber and driftwood. He told people that he was very proud of his workmanship and it had been sturdy enough to last him four winters, until now. Both men watched intently as their homes were destroyed. Aisha came over and stood between them and put her arms around them.

'So sorry guys,' said Aisha, 'but we were lucky - if you want to call it that - we just made it.' I've never seen anything like it in my life,' said Simon.

The huge Swede rubbed tears from his eyes. 'If it wasn't for you all - we might have been burned to death,' so thanks to you... from here.' he touched his heart.

'Yes, thank you both,' said Alfred. 'It's upsetting, but we can rebuild. It looks like it's destroyed the whole village, the fire breaks were not sufficient to hold it back. The power of nature... huh.'

'Do you have a family Alfred, a partner?' Aisha asked.

Alfred nodded. 'I've only just met someone, her name is Agnetha - it's early days - she has a small child.' he smiled - they left a few days ago. Most of the village has been relocated to the town, I think they are living in a school... temporarily, but we'll return - we're resilient people, eh Sven.'

'Better believe it my friend,' and he stepped forward and gave Alfred a massive hug.'She's a lovely girl by the way, wait 'til you meet her Aisha, a beauty - another Swede of course - we're taking over the island.' Everyone found time to smile.

The dawn was here now and they could see more clearly the devastation the fire had caused. as Panos started up the boat again and steered carefully around the rocky Cape and headed towards Neo Horio.

He slowed the boat right down and came to a halt in a deep bay. 'I'm stopping for a little while, we need a break. I'll put the kettle on,' he said.

'Great idea mate,' said Simon, putting his thumb up.

Panos cut the engine and dropped the small anchor. The sea was like a mirror. They were anchored under bleached white sea cliffs that towered above them.

'Isn't it beautiful?' Panos said. 'Even in tragedy there is beauty.'

Everyone joined him in the cabin, it was a bit of a squeeze.

'Yes mate, it's a beautiful place we live in and we've had a lucky escape,' said Simon.

'I'll never take all this for granted again,' Panos said, gesturing with his hand.

'I don't think any of us will Panos,' said Sven. Suddenly he started laughing.

'What's so funny, big man?' asked Simon.

'I've just noticed. Your faces are filthy, mine must be too. We look like coal miners.'

A ripple of laughter went round the boat. - as everyone looked at each other's faces.

'Have you contacted Mags yet Sven? I know it's early - but best to reassure her - news travels fast round here,' Simon said.

'I'll text her, I don't want to wake her,' said Sven.

'I'm not sure if she'll have slept much,' Aisha said.

'Alfred, how about you, have you been in touch with your girlfriend?'

'No, not thought about it in all the commotion - I'll text her now.

Panos and Aisha were busy sorting the teas and coffees out, and they handed them around. Everyone held their steaming mugs close to them.

Panos suddenly held his hand up. 'Wait one minute my friends, I nearly forgot.' He reached into a wooden cupboard and produced a large unopened bottle of rum. He opened it with relish and poured everyone a large tot into their hot drinks.

'Panos... you are a miracle man,' said Sven. 'What great timing you have.'

'Yeah - nice one mate,' said Simon, smiling broadly.

'It's a gift from the Gods,' smiled Panos.

'Here's to the Gods then and here's to friendship!' Simon shouted, lifting his mug in a toast.

'And life,' said Sven, quietly- 'here's to life.

15
THE HEROES RETURN

A small welcoming committee was gathered on the quayside - as they returned to port and the boat cut through a placid sea - in the cool November morning. Panos could see Eleni and his children waving excitedly jumping up and down and the diminutive figure of Mags stood beside them waving frantically too.

Panos expertly guided the boat alongside and Simon flung the forward ropes to Eleni, who grabbed them as Aisha flung the aft ones to Panos's son Dimitri and they tied them to the bollards.

'Kalimera! Your darling Papa and husband are home, make merry with the Ouzo!' Panos boomed, as he cut the engine and walked out of the cabin, then jumped off onto the jetty towards his wife and children, as they rushed towards him and enveloped him in a huge bear hug. Sven and Alfred leapt off the boat - and Sven stepped forward to meet the onrushing Mags, and lifted her up easily into his huge arms. Simon and Aisha were the last to get off, and stood on the quayside together - arm in arm, watching the scene unfold.

'Thank God you're safe,' said Eleni. Your faces are filthy. You've obviously not had time for a wash then?' she said, giggling.

'No my darling, we have been... a little bit busy,' Panos answered, smiling broadly.

'The stubborn Swede returns,' said Mags, holding Sven's hand tightly. 'Thank you so much my darlins - I owe you all several drinks for this.'

'Thank god you are all safely home. Come, we must get you some food and help you clean up,' said Eleni, beckoning them to her large four by four, parked on the quayside.

'I left my car here, thanks Eleni,' Simon said. 'We'll take Sven and Mags back to our place and join you at the taverna.'

'I must go and find Agnetha,' she'll be worried,' Alfred said.

'Tell us where you want to go and we'll drop you off,' Eleni said.

'Thank you so much,' Alfred replied.

Eleni and Panos dropped Alfred off in town.

Back at Simon's place, he and Aisha and Sven enjoyed a leisurely shower and spent ages scrubbing the soot off their faces.

'That feels better,' said Simon walking into the lounge with a towel around his neck. He'd changed into a clean pair of jeans and a t-shirt and flip flops.

Sven and Mags were sitting on the balcony in the mid morning sun, overlooking the harbour far below.

'Don't think you'll be going to the disco in those jeans any time soon Sven,' Simon remarked.

Sven laughed. 'Yes they are rather on the short side. Thanks for the loan though,' he said, stretching his huge long legs out in front of him for comic effect.

Aisha was in the kitchen, busy making coffee.

She shouted. 'Thought we'd have a coffee here before going over to the Taverna. Eleni will have a feast ready for us if I know her!'

'I'm starving - could eat a scabby horse,' said Simon.

Aisha walked in with a tray of coffees. 'Scabby horse?'

'It's Irish,' Simon explained.

'Thought it might be. You have some crazy expressions.'

'Everyone must be starving, we've not eaten properly since last night,' Simon said, rubbing his stomach. 'Hang on a minute. I've just thought of something, we've not let the Police and Fire Service know that we're safe? They could be looking for us, putting their lives at risk.'

Sven put his hand out. 'Relax my friend, Mags contacted them. I think they want to speak to us though,'

'I guess we can't complain - the Fire Chief gave us plenty of warning.'

'True,' said Sven.'

'Serves you daft buggers right,' said Mags, 'arsin around like that at your ages.'

Sven and Simon exchanged sheepish glances.

'And that goes for you too Aisha.' Mags continued.

Aisha giggled. 'I can't argue Mags, as I said, I blame the mad Irishman and the equally mad Viking, they've been watching too many films if you ask me.'

'Hey, that's rich. It was your idea to stay overnight, remember, instead of doing the sensible thing - and persuading them to come back with us the same day,' said Simon, putting his cup down on the table.

'Me? Never, you must have been thinking of someone else. Anyway - my female intuition must have worked - because we're all home safe,' Aisha replied.

***

Simon and Aisha and Mags and Sven arrived at the Taverna in the late morning and as Aisha had predicted, Eleni had set out a huge amount of food for them all, a mixture of Greek and English dishes.

'Please help yourself,' Eleni said, gesturing over to the tables groaning with food.

Panos was busy in the kitchen making coffee and heating up croissants. 'She's got me busy, as if I haven't been through enough, my friends.' Panos's loud voice echoed from the kitchen.

Simon went through to the kitchen doorway. 'You love it mate - you're in your natural home here, the Fire Chief said so himself.

Panos laughed. 'I hope he doesn't come looking for us, that's all.'

'I wouldn't bet on it mate, he wasn't very happy with us,' Simon replied.

Simon went back to the table and helped himself to several bacon rolls and wolfed into them. Everyone else did likewise.

'This is fantastic Eleni, thanks so much,' said Aisha.

'It's my pleasure,' she replied.

It went quiet for a while, as everyone busied themselves eating ravenously. Eleni sat down and drank her coffee and Panos came out of the kitchen with more croissants and sat beside her.

'What's the news mate. I see the smoke plume's gotten smaller,' Simon said, looking skyward.

Panos took a sip from his coffee. 'I spoke to a friend in the fire service earlier, they seem to have contained it, after it passed through Ayia Varvara and some of the other smaller coastal villages. So, we hope they're getting the better of it. I hear it's made the main news broadcasts. Thank God no one was injured or died.'

'Let's hope it's under control then, I wouldn't want anyone to go through what we went through,' said Simon.

'Me neither,' Sven agreed, 'even though it was our own choice.'

'Daft eejits, said Mags, ' You could have written yourself off and left me - a poor widow.'

Sven smiled. 'We're not married Mags, last time I looked anyway.'

'You know what I mean - you big Scandinavan fool.'

'I've nothing to leave you anyway little one,' Sven continued, 'I only had my cottage and my yurt, and they've both gone.' Sven shook his head.

'Here's a question,' Aisha said.

'Go on,' replied Sven.

'Insurance?'

The big man smiled. 'We're not great with things like insurance in Aya Varvara, we're hippies, remember, free spirits - we'll just have to start from scratch. We're a close little community, we'll all pitch in and help each other rebuild, not sure about the older folks though - they might have to move in with their families in Neo Horio - until it's safe.'

'Look out,' Panos said suddenly. 'We have company.'

Everyone turned to look in the direction of two figures in uniform, who were striding purposefully towards their table. Panos recognised the bulk of Dimitri the Fire Chief straight away. He was accompanied by a taller slighter figure and as they got closer Panos saw that it was the island's Police Chief Manolis Makriadis,who had been a few years above Panos in high school.

The two men stood back a few feet from the table. The tall thin man coughed.

'Good morning ladies and gentleman, we are very sorry to disturb your...celebrations.'

'Good morning,' everyone replied in a subdued chorus.

'Please take a seat,' Panos said, as he and Eleni stood up and quickly found chairs for the men to sit on.

'Would you like some coffee gentleman?' Eleni asked them.

'No thank you, we won't be staying long Eleni, the taller man replied.

The Police Chief shifted in his seat and sat up very straight, his gold buttons glinting in the late morning sun, against the blue serge of his dress jacket. He'd clearly made an effort. He had a rich deep voice and his face was a mask of sternness. He sat up stiffly in his chair, and pushed his chest out. 'I am Manolis Makriadis, in case any of you don't know me, I'm the Chief of Police for Xanthos. He pointed over towards his colleague. 'This is the Fire Service Chief Dimitri Dianeddes, I believe most of you have met him,' he said slowly and deliberately. Dimitri nodded.

'I believe you know why we are here, so I'll come straight to the point... By your reckless actions you put our brave firefighters and policemen and women's lives at risk over at Ayia Varvara.'

Sven interrupted. 'Please, do not include my friends, it was *me* who was stubborn and would not leave - they tried to persuade me to come with them, but I refused, I was pig-headed.'

The Police Chief put his hand up.

'Please Mr Olaffson, let us finish what we are going to say. Fire Chief, please continue.'

The Fire Chief nodded to his colleague. 'As you are aware, I spoke to you several times Mr Olaffson, and made you aware of the danger you were putting yourself in, not to mention my firefighters and the police... but you chose to ignore that advice. I also spoke to you and your friends on the day before your village caught fire and was later destroyed. And still none of you would leave. You could all have easily been killed that night, not to mention our brave workers, who tried to rescue you. We could not get near the village because of the smoke and flames. Luckily we had spotters out - who saw you all leave safely by boat early this morning. That by the way was pure luck and nothing else.'

The Police Chief interrupted. 'Excuse me Dimitri. What do you all have to say for yourselves, especially you Mr Olaffson?'

Sven ran his fingers through his blonde hair and wiped a sheen of sweat from his forehead. He looked around at the whole table, then focused on the Fire Chief and Police Chief. 'I am *so* sorry,' said Sven. 'I cannot begin to tell you how bad I feel, for putting your brave workers in danger and also for involving my friends in this.' He looked around and could hardly meet their eyes. 'I was stupid and also stubborn. I wanted to protect my property, but it was selfish and reckless of me. I can see that now.' He felt Mag's hand reassuring hand on his arm.

'I would like to try and do something to make amends for this.' He let out a long sigh, and took a swig of his coffee. Simon noticed that Sven's hands were shaking.

The silence hung in the air, everyone could feel the tenseness, no one wanted to speak for fear of saying the wrong thing.

The police chief addressed Sven - his face was flushed with anger.

'The best way *you* can make amends is to offer a public apology to the brave firemen and women and police men and women who are still out there risking their lives, saving people like you Mr Olaffson.'

Sven's face reddened. 'Of course, of course I will, It will be an honour. It could have turned out much worse, much worse.'

'You are correct, we could have charged you and you'd be standing in a criminal court in Neo Chorio right now, instead of sitting in these beautiful gardens, eating lovely food, and surrounded by your equally stubborn friends.'

'And now Mr McCardle, we need to mention your part in this unwise expedition. I believe you had good intentions, trying to help a friend - I am given to understand. However, it appears that you and your friends soon abandoned attempts to persuade Mr Olaffson to get in the boat with you and leave the area. You subsequently stayed the night at his cottage, despite my colleague the Fire Chief warning you all it would be risky and dangerous, not just for you and the people with you, but for the police and firefighters. If it wasn't for your friend here Miss Morrison.' He looked over towards Mags, who sat frozen in her chair. He continued. 'If it wasn't for her explaining that your actions were honourable, and that you, as a longstanding friend, were trying to help her, then *you* may also have been in trouble.'

Simon held both his hands up. 'You're dead right Chief. I have no excuse. We were only trying to help, but got caught up in it all. I'd like to apologise too, I'll do whatever it takes to make this better.'

Mags put her hand up. 'It was *me* that asked Simon and his friends to rescue Sven. I feel so guilty about that. They were only doing what I asked them, as a favour for a friend. I know we've not come out of it smelling of roses. I'm truly sorry for involving you all in this. Truly sorry.' Eleni passed Mags a tissue and she dabbed her reddened eyes.

There was a long uncomfortable silence and then the Police Chief and his colleague slowly stood up and the Police Chief drew himself up to his full height and bowed slightly.

We will bid you a very good morning ladies and gentleman. Thank you for your time. Please be careful in future. Oh... and Panos...try to knock some Greek sense into your friends please ...and save some for yourself while you are at it. Next time - if there is a next time, we will not be so forgiving.'

The sarcasm wasn't lost on Panos. He stood up. 'Yes of course Commissioner,' he said in almost a whisper. His booming voice for once was subdued.

He put his hand up in a weak gesture of goodbye, then slumped back in his chair, as the two officials began walking out of the Taverna gardens, towards their waiting staff cars.

Everyone turned to look at Panos. He let out a loud sigh and put his head in his hands.

'I don't know about anyone else - but I could do with a large Ouzo!' he said, surprisingly finding his voice again.

16

WINTER

Xanthos started to settle into its normal winter rhythms now that the forest fires had finally been extinguished. A local man had been arrested and charged with arson. The central government in Athens had donated a substantial sum of money from its emergency fund. This was to help the islanders rebuild their homes, but also to try and replant their olive groves, many of which had been owned by the same families for centuries. The islanders themselves had also set up a hardship fund, and donated food parcels and clothing to the young families and older residents who had suffered most in the fires.

Sven and his fellow villagers had already moved back to Agia Varvara to salvage what they could and began the arduous task of rebuilding their homes and also their lives, after the trauma of the fire. Panos's cousin Georgios and his builders had visited the village and kindly donated many offcuts of wood and also bags of cement and sand to help them. These were gratefully received. The younger, hardier villagers who were doing the rebuilding, slept in makeshift dwellings on the beach and the rest of the community lived in temporary accommodation in the town. It would probably be Spring before they could all move back properly. It was cold and damp for the builders in the early mornings and evenings, but thankfully warm and balmy during the day and the men and women who lived on the beach were young and fit. Georgios' building company and a few others on the island had been given government contracts - to help rebuild some of the houses that had been burnt down and they set to work immediately. The Winter storms could be brutal and they wanted to make the new properties as safe and warm as possible in the short window they had left.

***

Simon and Aisha sat in their kitchen, as the mid morning December sun streamed through the window. Simon was at his laptop, doing some writing.

'Have you heard back about your article about the fires yet?'

'Not yet, but I'm hopeful they'll publish it in the *Olive Press*, the expats and the locals read that. There's so much competition out there these days, what with twitter, facebook, blogs and the like, everyone fancies themselves as a journo.'

'I'm sure you'll hear soon.'

'The problem is, these sorts of articles need to be published quickly after the event or they lose their impact.'

'Yes, it's amazing how many people I've bumped into in the street who never mention it now, and it was only a few weeks ago,' said Aisha.

Simon took a sip of his coffee. 'Life goes on - everyone's talking about Christmas now, at least no one was injured or killed, although that fireman had bad smoke inhalation, thank god he's ok now though. Anyway it'll be a quiet one this year, no big party at Panos and Elenis - they're going to Rhodes to see his brother. So, what are we up to today then? It feels a bit flat after all the excitement.'

'You live on adrenaline too much, you should try meditation, it really works,' said Aisha.

'Tried it once, fell asleep.'

'Aargh, you really are a frustrating man.'

'I know, but you love me.'

'Not when you drag me on one of your mad escapades.'

'Got to help out friends in need,' he replied. 'It may be us one day.'

'Yes I know, I hope not though,' Aisha said, as she got up from her chair and walked towards the window that overlooked the harbour and beyond to the mountain range.

She sat back down next to him. 'Hiking,' said Aisha

'You have a butterfly mind. Hiking, what about it?'

'We should go, there are so many beautiful mountains here. I used to do it all the time back home - get away from everything, people, and it's great exercise. It's been a bit mad recently.'

'Just a bit. It's been a while since I've done any myself.'

She got up again and walked towards the bookcase and bent down to rummage around for a bit. 'Found it.' She held up a map of the island.

'That's a tourist map, we need a proper, detailed one.'

'It'll do for now.'

'Ok, let's have a look.'

Simon made a pot of fresh coffee and they sat down on the couch in the lounge and pored over the map. 'We'll have to be careful, some places are still no- go areas, due to the fire damage. The olive groves will need to be replanted and we can't walk over the burnt areas due to erosion, it takes years to grow back properly they say,' Simon said.

'I don't see a problem if we pick our spot carefully,' Aisha replied.

'How about Mount Ariadne, at just over 600 metres, or 2000 feet if you like,' he said, pointing to the largest peak on the island. 'It's well away from where the fires were, it should be safe enough.'

'It's ambitious, but it looks good. We should go in the next few days,' Aisha said. 'We can always turn back if it gets too much. We'll have to start early though as there's not that much daylight.'

'You're on. I need some new boots though.'

Simon tried on several hiking boots in the shop. It was mainly a camping shop, but they sold other stuff too, quite unusual for a small island. Some locals had spotted an opportunity for the new trend for camping and walking holidays and a clever young couple had opened the shop up a few months earlier. It was also one of the few shops in the town that remained open in Winter, as many of the tourists liked to visit during the off season, as the walking and camping weather was much cooler.

He finally settled on a pair of fancy and expensive all weather boots, much to Aisha's relief.

'I thought we were going to be here all day,' she said

'Need to get the right boots, eh Manos,' he said looking at the shop owner, a young man in his late twenties with an impressively long and trendy beard. Simon knew him from a navigation course he'd done a couple of years back.

'Absolutely Simon, boots are an important purchase. Where are you thinking of going then?'

'Mount Ariadne,' Simon replied.

'Ah, great choice, it should be quiet this time of year, although we're getting people all year round now, since we started the business. It's due to the mild Winters here and also people are getting a bit tired of the big touristy islands, they want to get away from it all and that's difficult on the more busy islands.'

'That's great news Manos, it's good to see some entrepreneurs starting businesses and keeps you young ones here, instead of moving away to the mainland,' said Aisha.

'Thanks Aisha, yes we're very happy to stay here and raise our families. It's beginning to revitalise the island. There's lots of opportunities for other stuff too. He motioned over to his wife Maria who was standing at the counter, who waved. We're thinking of starting sea kayaking courses and walking holidays too.'

'Wow, that's great news mate. If you need help with a website or writing any articles in the local press or whatever, give me a shout. Mates rates,' said Simon.

'That's kind of you, I'll certainly bear that in my mind.'

They left the shop with beaming smiles and Simon's new boots and laden with lots of other stuff neither of them had planned to buy. Simon held up his bags. 'We'd better start using this stuff then, to get our money's worth.'

'No better time than to start than now, well tomorrow I mean, can't wait,' Aisha replied.

'First though, a coffee at Marios,' said Simon.

Marios's was quiet this lunchtime. A few locals and expats were sitting around. Most were clad in woollen jumpers and light outdoor jackets - as the weather had turned colder the last few days. The sun was still strong though and people welcomed the peace and calmness, after the hectic tourist season.

'This is the life eh,' said Simon, putting his arm around Aisha's shoulder.

'Not bad for December. It's cold where my sister lives. She texted me while we were in the shop. They've had heavy snow and some roads are blocked, she said.'

'They can keep that, I prefer the warmth. I've made some bad choices sometimes in my life - coming to live here - was definitely one of my better ones. Pass me that guidebook, will you darling,' Simon said.

17
THE MOUNTAIN WALK

They parked in the small car park at the foot of Mount Ariadne at around seven thirty, just as it got light. No one else was there at that early hour. They'd chosen quite a well used route. The locals sometimes thought tourists were a bit mad to be attempting to climb mountains. Simon had completed the trek a few years ago on his own and was looking forward to reacquainting himself. They were rewarded with a beautiful sunny morning, although it would take a while to warm up.

'What a day,' Aisha said, as she swung her backpack over her shoulders and adjusted the straps. Her breath was smokey in the morning air.

'Amazing,' Simon replied. 'We live in an incredible place.'

'How's the new boots?' Aisha asked.

'I'll let you know in a couple of hours. I've taped up the hot spots - but I may still get a few blisters.'

'See how you go, you can check when we stop for coffee.'

Simon locked the car and they did a few last minute checks and then set off up the track towards the pine clad forest.

After about an hour they were out of the forest and climbing steeply into a glade of pencil-like cypress trees. Someone had made a bench from some bleached old olive wood and they both sat down, glad of the break.

Simon was breathing heavily and let out a weary sigh. 'I'm not quite as fit as I thought I was, I'm knackered already.'

'Knackered, that means tired - yes?' Aisha smiled.

'Yes I forget sometimes - because your English is excellent - but it's a strange word.'

'Coffee break?' Aisha asked.

'Why not.'

Aisha took off her gloves and reached into her rucksack and pulled out a gleaming new flask and carefully poured two cups of steaming coffee.

Simon took a sip. 'Ah that's hit the spot, any biscuits?'

Aisha handed him a foil wrapped chocolate biscuit from her bag and he demolished it quickly.

'I told you we should have had breakfast,' she said.

'Too early for me. All I want is coffee at that ungodly hour.'

'Some view eh?' said Aisha.

Simon pointed out to sea. 'Yes, that bit of land you can see in the far distance is the west coast of Crete, it looks quite close, but it's about forty miles away. It's quite unusual to see it, but the light's so clear today.

'Looks amazing,' said Aisha. 'As well as my recent visit - I went there once before, in my twenties, backpacking with a girlfriend. We went for three months - what an adventure - we stayed at a little fishing village. It was so cheap in those days and everything was unspoiled, there were hardly any tourists. We weren't looking at antiquities back then - I can assure you.' She smiled. 'When I went back last year - lots of memories came back. Some of the things we got up to. If my parents knew.'

'I can imagine. I did something similar in the early eighties . I went to the island of Hydra with my girlfriend at the time. Her name was Patricia O'Malley, she had flame red hair. We thought we were following in the footsteps of Leonard Cohen and all that. I fancied myself as a bit of a poet back then, living the bohemian lifestyle and she was going to be my Marianne. We were both dreamers.'

'And how did that work out?'

'We made a kind of pilgrimage - to Cohen's old house, it wasn't that easy to find, it was tucked away in a winding backstreet and not quite what we expected. I thought there'd be a plaque or something, but it was just like any other little island house. Some people had left mementos, withered flowers and faded black and white photos of the man himself were stuck to the door. There were a few older locals there who remembered him and his friends - but time had moved on and so had they. We were a bit disappointed. I don't think he'd been back there since the seventies. I loved his music - I still do - it's a shame he died quite recently. One of the locals told me that some of Cohen's family still used it from time to time. We stayed for a few days. I wrote a couple of daft romantic poems and then we got the ferry back to Athens.'

'And your girlfriend, with the red hair - the would be Marianne, what became of her?'

'We split up not long after we got back. I heard later she'd married an insurance clerk, so much for the bohemian lifestyle.'

Aisha smiled. 'It's strange where we end up in life. You start off thinking you're going down one path - then the path changes and you end up nowhere near where you thought you were going to be.'

'Sounds about right,' Simon said. 'Shall we go?'

The path ascended steeply until they came to a rocky outcrop, providing stupendous views over the sparkling sea. Some fishing boats were out at sea - but all the tourist craft and ferries had stopped for the Winter.

'Those boats remind me of the fires a few weeks ago - I guess we were pretty stupid, attempting that sort of thing at our age,' said Aisha, as she admired the view.

'Ha. You're younger than me, I'll be sixty in four years, I can't believe it,' Simon replied.

'You've been coming here for many years. Do you think of Xanthos as your home now?'

Simon sat down on a rock and thought about it. 'Yes I suppose I do.'

'I can see why you love it so much. I'm beginning to feel that way myself.'

'Do you ever think about going back - to Northern Ireland I mean - you must have friends there.'

'Not really - I left there when I was young. I've lived longer in London than Belfast.'

'Timecheck?' she asked

'We've been going for two hours and it'll soon be time for lunch. We'll reach the summit in an hour and a half at this rate. Wait 'til you see the old monastery, it's an amazing sight.'

'I'm looking forward to it.'

They rounded a bend just before 10 o'clock and caught sight of the ruined Greek Orthodox monastery of St John The Theologian, perched precariously on the edge of a cliff. The sun was coming out - although because of the altitude, the temperature had dropped a few degrees from ground level. They reached the front of the old monastery and stood before the huge arched entrance, and took in the centuries of decay. It looked neglected and unloved. The once honey coloured sandstone stone was weathered black in places and was crumbling away quite badly at some points. It had been a three storey building and the bell tower sat above the entrance. The bell had long since gone and pigeons now roosted noisily in the tower. You could see it had been a very impressive building at one time and its red tiled roof framed a huge central courtyard. There were weeds growing from every crevice and the cry of the birds sounded eerie in the morning air.

'Aisha stood back and admired the sight. 'Wow, who would have thought you'd find this all the way up here?'

'A hidden gem, far from the world and its earthly temptations. It's over five hundred years old,' said Simon. 'It's been added to over the years of course, it's hard to tell where the original building ends and the modern buildings begin. It was a working monastery until the nineteen seventies apparently,' he continued. 'Fifty monks lived all their lives here…and died here too of course, most of them never visited the town. They had to pull up all their supplies by ropes and baskets from the cliff edge and later, supplies were carried up by donkey. It must have been a simple but hard life in some ways, very self sufficient, they grew all their own vegetables and kept livestock too. Come, we'll look around.' He put his arm around her and led her through the gloomy archway.

They picked their way carefully along the ancient path. 'No pleasures of the flesh then,' she smiled.

'Oh no, none of that, vows of celibacy and all that - they gave all their energy to God.'

'I'm very impressed by your knowledge. How come you know so much about it?'

He pointed over to a notice board a few yards away. 'I've just read it from that plaque over there. Only joking. I did an article about it for the Xanthos Tourist Board a few years ago, so I had to research it. That must have been the last time I was here. It was ten years ago, come to think of it. Where did that go? I've heard that there's plans to start renovating it. It should be treasured, if they want to honour the monks' memories and bring a better class of tourist here too.'

They began to explore some of the old rooms, most of the doors had been stolen for firewood by the locals many years ago. Some of the old prayer rooms and monks' cells were relatively intact, although they smelt damp and musty and had water running down the walls. More birds were nesting in the roof space of the main chapel which was just an empty shell now and they flew away with a noisy flurry out of the open roof, when Simon and Aisha entered.

'It's a bit creepy but you can imagine what it was like all those years ago. We have similar monasteries in Bosnia, Orthodox too of course.'

'Yes, they must have been pretty special people to want to live their entire lives here though, with just each other for company.'

'A very simple life, wonder if they ever argued?' she said.

'I'm pretty sure they would have, they were human beings not saints. You couldn't become a saint until you died of course.'

'I won't hold my breath for you then,' she giggled.

'Ha, no I wouldn't if I were you, although I think Irish saints were a bit more human, liked a drink or two perhaps. Although the guys that lived here brewed their own beer and raki apparently. They had to have some pleasures.'

'Wild parties eh,' said Aisha.

'Probably a bit of high spirits, if you'll excuse the pun.'

After a bit more exploring they walked out of the old ruins and further up the path and off the track and down the hill to a large flat area, with far reaching views over the sea.

'Good spot for lunch?' he asked, taking his rucksack off and laying it down.

'Wonderful.' Aisha took hers off too and laid it on a big rock.

She looked around. 'This looks man-made. Why so flat I wonder, foundations for more buildings perhaps?'

'Graveyard,' Simon replied.

'Graveyard?' She looked shocked. 'Should we be standing here, it's sacrilege, no?'

'Relax, this was never used. The main graveyard is down there in that dip.' he said, pointing to a hollowed out area in the valley about two hundred yards away. The monastery was abandoned before this land could be used for more graves, apparently.'

'The main graveyard was getting full up and the monks dug this bit out for the future. I bet they never thought tourists like us would use it for a picnic area.'

'Let's have a look before lunch,' he said.

They walked down the slope to the graveyard. There were hundreds of graves in various stages of decay, most had fallen over. They examined the first one they came to. It was still upright and larger than the rest and more well cared for..

Papa Kyriakos - The Patriarch - 1880 - 1965 - May his soul rest in eternal peace.

'Kyriakos, that means Sunday doesn't it?' Aisha asked.

'Correct - lots of the priests were named after the holy day. Looks like he was the head monk at that time, your main man.'

Aisha walked on a little further. 'Here look at this one.' She bent down to have a better look.

'Brother Pavlos Andronikos The Gentle One 1820 - 1903.' How touching.

'Yes it is. Like I said, it was a strange way of life, peaceful mind you, but their choice I guess. Living all the way up here nearer to God, oblivious to the fleshpots of the town below.'

'Wouldn't have suited you though darling,' Aisha replied.

'Or you.' he smiled.

'Let's leave them in eternal peace, as they say. We have a lot of living to do,' Simon said and they turned to walk back up the hill.

They put down their rucksacks and placed a blanket on the ground and Aisha began setting out lunch.'

'What we got?' he asked.

'Of course you wouldn't know, you were still snoring when I got up extra early to prepare this.'

'Ha - need my beauty sleep and all that eh.'

She undid various jars and packets and set out bowls of olives, sun dried tomatoes, fresh bread and a wonderful salad made with fresh beefsteak tomatoes, onions and cucumbers and salty feta. There was also ham and meatballs, and various other tasty side dishes.

'That's amazing, smells fantastic too, I'm starving.'

She filled a paper plate up, and handed it to him with a plastic knife and fork and a napkin.'

'Thanks.'

'Oh I nearly forgot, we have soup,' she said, reaching back into her rucksack, and pulled a large flask out and opened it and the scent of garlic filled the air as she poured steaming hot lentil and lamb soup into the cups and handed one to Simon. He blew on it and took a sip.

'Mmm that is delicious, spicy too.'

'You can thank Eleni, she gave me the recipe - her grandmothers. Here, have some bread.'

They ate in companionable silence, admiring the incredible views and taking in the peace and serenity.

'Grand feast you made there - quite the chef eh.'

'I enjoy cooking. I find it relaxing.'

'I'll have to give you the recipe for my grannie's Irish Stew, if I can remember it.'

'I'll look forward to that.'

They were soon on their way again and had to stop several times on the final part of the ascent, and after some arduous climbing, they finally reached the summit at around 11am. There was a small metal plaque on top which glinted in the sun, it said *Mount Ariadne - 600 metres. The highest summit on the Island of Xanthos.* There was a little stylised map which showed Xanthos in relation to the other nearby islands.

They were both breathing very heavily and gave each other beaming smiles. '*Yessss* - we did it!' Simon said - as they hugged each other in triumph. 'Well done us, what a climb.'

Aisha was still trying to catch her breath. 'It was well worth it. What amazing views.' She pointed out to sea. 'You can see Crete much clearer now, you're right though, it looks within touching distance.'

He reached into his rucksack and took out two small bottles of beer and opened them, the beer fizzed over the top of the bottle from its bumpy journey up the mountain. He handed one to Aisha.

Simon lifted his bottle. 'Yammas.'

'Yammas,' replied Aisha - clinking bottles together.

'We'll go back to the taverna and celebrate and make Panos jealous. He's been here all his life and never climbed this, the lazy bugger.'

18

THE KALLIKANTZAROS

The Taverna was only open for the sale of teas and coffees and cakes and pastries, as they had long since closed to tourists for the season. Panos and Eleni were sitting at the big table enjoying a mid afternoon coffee.

'Kalispera,' Panos shouted, as he had spotted Simon and Aisha getting out of their car. 'Where have you been my friends?'

Simon and Aisha sat down at the table with them. 'We've just climbed Mount Ariadne,' Aisha said proudly, with a beaming smile.

'What - oh my god - are you two crazy, it's thousands of feet high. It's nearer the Gods of Mount Olympus than the ground - you are both mad.'

'Oh Panos - stop exaggerating. Good for you two,' said Eleni. 'I climbed it with my father once, I must have been about fourteen, I thought it was never going to end. I complained the whole way up - and down.'

'It *was* pretty tough to be honest - a lot harder than we realised. We discovered we're not as fit as we thought either,' said Asha.

'Yeah it was bloody hard actually mate- are you telling me the truth when you said you've never been up there?' Simon asked.

Pans patted his large belly. 'Do I look like I'm built to be a mountaineer?'

'Well, come to think of it mate,' Simon laughed.

'I'm keeping quiet,' said Eleni, smiling, as she got up from the table. 'Two coffees, yes?'

'Thanks Eleni,' Aisha replied.

'You'll be looking forward to your trip to Rhodes for Christmas,' said Aisha.

'Of course, only ten days now, it's been ages since I saw Dimitri.'

'He owns a hotel doesn't he?' asked Aisha.

'Yes, a big fancy one in Lindos - one of the main tourist resorts - it's a lot of work, but he has a lot of good staff. He and his wife Maria are very hands on though.'

'Is he older or younger than you?' Aisha continued, as Eleni set down two coffees for her and Simon.

'Older - fifty five. I keep telling him to retire, so does Maria - he's made his money but he won't listen, he likes to be involved - like I said, he'd be very bored if he retired. I'm the same. We've inherited this mad work obsession from our father - he rarely had a break - he was never away from this place.'

Simon took a sip from his coffee and leaned back in his chair. 'I must admit the prospect of retiring doesn't exactly fill *me* with delight either. He'll not be short of business in Rhodes - a beautiful island. Aisha and I were talking earlier about the other islands we'd visited. I've been to Rhodes, I stayed at Lindos, Pefkos too - that was a bit quieter, it was many moons ago. I really loved Lindos, very busy though, and so pretty with all those narrow cobbled streets and open air restaurants, the beaches were amazing too - St Pauls Bay I remember.'

Eleni fetched the coffee pot and gave everyone refills. 'What's your plans for Xmas then?' she asked.

'Grant and Jude have asked us over for Christmas Day. They put on a brilliant feast,' Simon said.

'We're looking forward to being spoiled by someone else too,' said Eleni. 'We're so used to looking after other people.'

'You both deserve it,' said Aisha, 'and the kids will love it too. Does your brother have any kids, Panos?'

'Yes, two, like us - a boy eighteen and a girl twenty, they get on great with our two, they can't wait.'

Eleni gave a sigh. 'I miss the old days - proper Christmases, traditional ones.'

Simon put his cup down. 'I remember years ago, you invited Siobhan and I for Christmas. Dimitri and Roula were only small. I remember Panos and his Dad used to frighten them with tales of Goblins and stuff.'

'That sounds scary,' said Aisha.

Eleni smiled. 'It's an old Greek tradition really. The Goblins - as Simon called them - are *Kallikantzaroi* in Greek. They are short, fat ugly creatures.'

'Like someone else we know!' Simon pointed at Panos - quick as a flash - as he burst out laughing, along with everyone else, including Panos, who rolled up a paper sugar sachet and fired it at Simon, who ducked.

'Hey, I thought you were my friend. I'm not *that* ugly or Eleni wouldn't have married me.'

'Sorry mate, couldn't resist it.'

Eleni still had her hands over her face stifling her giggles. 'True my darling and you can take a joke against yourself, that's just one of the reasons I married you. Now ... where was I? Oh yes, the Kallikantzaros. Well...it is said that they live at the centre of the earth and every Xmas they come up to the surface, and cause mischief in every town and village all over Greece - and steal food and stuff. We used to burn a huge log in the fireplace for the twelve days of Christmas to keep them away. It would burn 'til the sixth of January when the Goblins would return to the centre of the earth. I remember my mother and father telling me about them when I was a child - it used to terrify me and my brothers.'

'No wonder, I'm scared myself just thinking about them,' said Aisha. 'We have something similar in Bosnia except they are Elves and they cause trouble and mischief - and steal food and stuff just like your ones. I used to love hearing about them, even though I was scared out of my wits.'

'What about you Simon?' Eleni asked, 'any goblins in Ireland?'

Simon sat forward and took a sip of his coffee.

'Well, let me see now, we don't have goblins as such, but we have Leprechauns, the *little people* we call them - like pixies . I guess that's our equivalent. They look like miniature people - and get up to mischief and stuff. They live at the bottom of peoples gardens and in glades in the woods. A lot of people actually believe in them, mainly the older generation. It's not just a Xmas thing, they're kind of all year round. What I remember most about Xmases growing up is going to Midnight Mass - or rather being dragged there by my parents. It's a big event in the Catholic church, not so much now - but it still happens. People used to go who hadn't been to church for years, and they usually reeked of booze - as they'd been in the pub all night.' Simon smiled ... 'They were the ones that used to see the Leprechauns - hence the saying ... *away with the fairies*.'

***

It was a few days before Xmas, and Simon and Aisha had put up their tree and were decorating the house. These rituals had got Simon thinking about his boyhood in Ireland. There were some real characters in those days, where he grew up, proper old school men and women, who would visit his mother and father over the Xmas and New Year period and always did a turn, sang a song, or played an instrument. His mother always welcomed them as it gave her a chance to join in. She was a great singer and dancer too and loved the parties that went on. His father seemed to tolerate them more than enjoy them.

He and Aisha sat down for a coffee together.

'I was just thinking about this time of year when I was growing up. I remember old Ma McCutcheon, who played the spoons, she had only one front tooth and two bottom ones and despite being called old Ma she was probably only in her fifties.

Aisha smiled.

'Then there was Kevin Connelly, who had a beautiful baritone voice - he went on to become quite a famous singer in Ireland. And Molly Kelly, the Irish dancer, who had luxurious auburn hair and a slim figure - she must have been about eighteen back then and me and the other teenage boys couldn't take their eyes off her. Jim O'Brian was one of them - a great mate of Simons - and a fantastic footballer. He had trials for Manchester United - but never quite made it professionally. He joined the British Army and I heard that he'd been killed by an IRA sniper when he was only twenty three. Sorry to ramble on, it's the time of year that we remember people.'

'I understand,' said Aisha. It's good to remember old times and good friends.'

'Well, I'm pretty sure that this Christmas is going to be better than last year - it was just *me* then. Panos and Eleni had invited me over of course - but my heart wasn't in it, and I didn't want to be a misery guts at their house, especially with their children there. New Year was the same. I hid away with a couple of bottles of Jameson's. What did you do?'

'I was still in Crete. I spent Christmas Day on my own - in a big soulless hotel, but I got through it.

Simon reached over and put his hand over hers. 'Well, let's hope this Christmas is better for both of us.'

She smiled. 'I'm sure it will.' She moved closer. 'Can we talk about something that's important to me?' Aisha said.

'Of course - this sounds serious though,' he replied.

'It is, though in a good way I hope. You know I spoke some time back about being a bit bored and wanting to do something, but I wasn't sure what it was?'

'Yes of course I do. When you came back from visiting your family.'

'Yes. I put it down to travelling and being a bit restless and the trial and everything, and I didn't want to seem ungrateful after all you and your friends have done for me.

'I told you I had trained as a yoga teacher back home and wanted maybe to take a more spiritual direction in life?'

'Yes I do. I told you I spotted your yoga mat in your courtyard when I came to visit that time. So you want to teach yoga?'

'There's a bit more to it. I've decided that I definitely don't want to go back to my University work any more. I'm burned out with it. I've been doing it for a long time. I've been thinking about it for some time. I spoke to my manager at the University yesterday and he said that I could still go for voluntary redundancy. I'd get a decent lump sum and a pension like I said a while back and I'd be independent again, and not have to live off you. Sorry, I should have mentioned this before. I just wanted to be sure in my own mind. I mentioned yoga. but I'm thinking a bit bigger than that. I've had quite a lot of counselling and therapy over the last few years - because of what I'd gone through. It was very healing and I've been thinking - I'd love to open a retreat here on the island. It's so beautiful and peaceful. It would be a place of creativity and healing - for people who have suffered, who need a place to relax or to learn new skills... we could also do Art and walking holidays and other stuff. Tell me what you're thinking? Am I mad?'

Simon put his coffee cup down and leaned forward in his chair 'Well - that's thrown me a curve ball for sure. No of course I don't think you're mad - far from it. I think it's a great idea, I really do. It needs a bit of thinking through though. He took a sip from his coffee. 'I went to a retreat in Spain a few years ago. I was going through a bit of a tough time after my dad died - and other stuff from my past. It was a great week - I loved it. I didn't think I would. I met some amazing people too. I kept meaning to go back but life somehow overtook me. I could have done with some of that calmness when I had that run in with Ruthven. I'm still annoyed with myself that I lost my temper.'

'Anger is a powerful emotion,' said Aisha. 'We can all learn lessons from life.'

'Yes I guess we can. What are you thinking - buy a plot or an old house you could renovate? Or we could build something here, we've acres of space in the garden. What a place for a retreat - in the olive grove. My god, you've got *me* excited now.'

Aisha smiled,' I wasn't sure how you'd take it. I thought you might think it was a crazy dream. I know we have to be practical too but I'll have the money from my redundancy. I wouldn't expect you to pay anything.'

'I'd love to help if I could, you know I don't have a lot of cash - but you can have the land, it's a fantastic idea.'

'That's so kind of you. I know that you wanted to sell this house at some point, but maybe this is a way of keeping it. We could look at some plots or old houses on the island too - we can speak to Georgios. It would be a proper business of course - we'd have to keep our feet on the ground - to make money to keep it going, and pay ourselves a salary - but we can work out these details. I feel so happy.' She smiled and put her arms around him. 'Thank you, you lovely man.'

19
GEORGIOS THE BUILDER

Georgios called and told them he'd found a large old house in a nearby village that might be suitable. They'd just got back from swimming at Agia Katerina Bay. The water was still warm, although maybe not for the locals. Xanthos was quite far south and enjoyed mild winters - although a dusting of snow sometimes fell on Mount Ariadne.

They sat in their lush garden, sipping coffee in the mid-morning sun.

'I'm so looking forward to seeing the house. It looks like Georgios has found a good one, it's quite near the beach too and accessible for town,' Simon said.

'Me too. I can't wait. Just one question though. Don't the locals object to us foreigners buying land here?

Simon paused to think before replying... 'Good point, depends on who you talk to though. Same as anywhere else I suppose. If you've been coming here for a long time and they trust you and you've put something back into the island economy and given work to the locals, - well then it's not a problem generally. I remember when Siobhan and I first started inquiring about buying a plot a few years ago-there were some locals who weren't very happy, but to be fair they were in the minority and it was the usual moaners of course - the ones who complain about everything. When we built the house, it gave Georgios and his men work for over a year, and they knew we were going to live here and most people knew us by then anyway.'

'That's good, ' Aisha said. 'I guess I worry too much.'

Simon smiled. 'It's normal to worry. It's a big project we're taking on.' Remember though, if all else fails - we still have this place.

'I know, but it's like we said, ideally we need a house separate from our business,' Aisha said.

'But it's reassuring to have the option isn't it?'

Time passed agonisingly slowly the morning of the viewing, but eventually twelve thirty came and they drove the short distance over to the small hamlet of Karillas. It stood on a steep hill overlooking the sea. They passed the remains of an old fort, which must have protected the village from marauding pirates in days gone by. There were around twenty houses and a population of roughly thirty. Most of the young ones had left home to work in Athens or moved into town to work in tourism, leaving the older folk, many of whose families had lived here for generations.

'Wonder why we've never been to this part of the island, it's not that far away from our house,' Aisha said as they drove into the village passing the old bakery, which used to serve everyone in the village.

'Dunno,' Simon replied. 'I've driven past here plenty of times but never stopped to explore. That fort must be at least four hundred years old. It's a pretty village and not too far to drive down to the beach, and it's a less touristy part of the island and because the beach is not right on the doorstep I guess there's not been much development.'

They spotted Georgios and stopped at the walled entrance to an olive grove, with a track leading a few hundred yards to an old abandoned house. He was leaning on a rusty gate and waved to them. They got out of the car and walked over to shake hands. Georgios held his umpteenth cigarette of the morning in his other hand.

'Good Morning. How are you both on this beautiful day?'

'All good thanks mate and you?' said Simon.

'I am well thank you.'

'And how is business these days. Plenty of work on I'll bet?'

'It keeps the wolf from the door,' he said smiling broadly.

'Come we will have a look.' He beckoned them over to the dilapidated house. Georgios told them that the house belonged to a family his father knew. It had been added to over the years as the size of their family had increased. When the old grandmother had died a few years ago it had been left to decay, as none of the younger members of the family wanted to live there. They considered it too old fashioned and it needed a lot of work done to modernise it.

They picked their way carefully through the dusty rooms and Simon was aware that they were treading over someone's past life and memories. All the furniture had been taken out but you could get a good idea about the size of the rooms.

'Be careful on the steps, they're rotting away,' Georgios said, as he led them both upstairs and opened the door to a large room at the back of the house, with a broken window. It was covered in cobwebs.

'Wait 'til you both see this,' he said pulling at the old window catch as it began to open with a creaking sound, and finally he had it fully open. The harsh afternoon light streamed into the room and Simon poked his head through the open window.

'Wow, now that's some view there. You can see right over the bay and across to the small islands, come have a look Aisha.'

'Oh my goodness, that's so beautiful, it's stunning, this will be a great place for someone to wake up to every morning with that view.'

'I knew you'd like it,' Georgios said.

They spent the next hour exploring the little cottage. There were five large rooms in all and an outbuilding set in another huge olive grove that tumbled down steeply toward the sea. They dusted off some old garden chairs and sat down at an equally old wickerwork table in the shade.

'So, what do you think? Georgios asked.

'I'll be honest Georgios I'm thinking why haven't you snapped this amazing place up for yourself? I don't mean to be rude,' Simon said.

'You're not rude, we are Greek, we like to talk straight. I was very tempted, I admit, but I have so much work at the moment. He paused to light another cigarette. There is a slight complication though... after all this is Greece, nothing is straightforward. There are quite a few family members who have a share in this house. it's the normal way of things here on the islands as you know. Everyone wants their share. By the way, the asking price is 75,000 euros'

'Bloody hell!' Simon exclaimed. 'for an old cottage. It's out of our league mate.'

'I don't think we can afford that,' Aisha said, looking crestfallen.

Georgios put his hand up to interrupt. 'Wait my friends, Siga Siga, take it slowly. Firstly, you have not seen the grounds yet. You could build at least another three houses on it, if you want -there is so much land.' He slowly lit another cigarette - drew deeply on it and blew a spiral of smoke upwards. 'Secondly - this is the *tourist* price, not the *real* price. I said earlier we must be patient. Leave it to old Georgios, it's a delicate issue and we have to tread carefully and we have also to keep the identity of the buyers as much a secret as possible.' He tapped his nose theatrically..

'Ok. But why is that, or am I being naive?' she asked.

Simon sighed. 'Darling, If the family gets to know that foreigners, that's us by the way, want to buy the house, then suddenly - the price shoots up and we're pushed out of the market.'.

'Simon is correct.' Georgios' eyes narrowed. 'We have to be like the cat and the mouse, we have to wait until the time is right to strike. Patience is a virtue the world over, and it is no different here in Greece.'

Simon smiled. 'I can't begin to tell you how much we appreciate this. You could have bought this place for yourself and made a good profit, it's so kind of you.'

'It's my pleasure Simon, you have always been a good friend to Panos and when he told me you were looking for a place to build your retreat, I was glad to be able to help.'

Simon shook hands warmly with Georgios. 'Thanks so much.'

Aisha offered him a handshake. 'Thanks Georgios.'

Georgios bowed. 'My pleasure.'

'So...to practicalities,' Simon said. 'How much work needs done and rough timescales etc?'

Georgios reached into his pocket and took out a crumpled piece of paper, and with great ceremony he unfolded it and smoothed out the creases with his hand on the table. He smiled broadly. 'As you can see, I've done a spreadsheet,' he said solemnly. Simon and Aisha suppressed their giggles.

'It'll be January soon and taking into account the weather delays, we *could* finish it in four to six months. You'll need an architect of course. I can sort that if you want. Once we have the proper drawings, I can give you a much clearer timescale. Does that sound ok?'

'Sounds good. We're not in a rush, but it would be nice to be ready for the tourist season, then we can begin to take in some income,' Aisha replied.

Georgios put his hand gently on her shoulder. 'As I said - leave it to old Georgios. I will do my very best.'

20
SHARING GOOD NEWS

Simon and Aisha entered the taverna garden and walked over towards the big table where Panos and Eleni were sitting. Simon ducked as he passed through the hanging vines above the tables.

'Good morning to you and to what do we owe pleasure so early?' boomed Panos.

Eleni looked over and smiled as they approached. Panos was sitting down polishing cutlery, whilst Eleni was folding tablecloths.

'Good morning. We just thought we'd pop by, it's been a while since we saw you both. How's business doing mate?'

'Not bad really, the season seems to get longer every year, we still have some tourists but it's mainly locals now. We're closing up tomorrow for the Winter. We've made enough this year, one of our best years actually, eh my darling.'

'Yes we can't complain, it's been a great year, but tiring though. We're looking forward to our Christmas trip to Rhodes,' Eleni replied. 'It'll be good to have a break.'

'What about you two? asked Eleni, 'Any plans for the New Year?'

'Well,' Simon hesitated… 'We might just have a special project. Or should I say Aisha has some big plans - to keep us occupied next year. I'll let her tell you - it's her baby.'

Eleni brought over two mugs and poured them a coffee each. 'Really, how intriguing - please tell us more.'

'Yes please do,' said Panos.

'I'm surprised Georgios hasn't mentioned it to you, although it's a rather sensitive,' Aisha said.

'I've not seen Georgios for ages. I've been too busy and he seems to have a lot of work on at the moment too, so our paths haven't really crossed. What's the big mystery then, you know what I'm like - I need to know what's going on in my little island?' Panos said.

Simon laughed. 'Yes I know you do mate, that's why we've kept it quiet from the Xanthos Gazette - otherwise known as Panayiotis Vasilliou.'

Eleni sighed. 'Leave them alone Panos, you are far too nosey.'

Panos looked suitably chastened. It didn't deter him though. 'All I'm saying is I should know about the comings and goings on my own island, especially when it's to do with our friends.'

Aisha took a sip of her coffee. 'I've been thinking about changing my career for a while. I've been doing the same job for many years. I want to try something different... I'd like to build a retreat - a special place, where people can come and relax - and maybe learn some new skills - like yoga, creative writing and maybe some painting holidays, walking, canoeing and outdoor stuff - a mixture of things. The young couple in the camping shop already run some of these holidays. We could get them involved.'

'That sounds fantastic,' said Eleni. What a wonderful idea. A place to come and relax and meditate maybe.'

'A place for the hippies,' Panos added mischievously.

'Perhaps,' Aisha replied, smiling.

SImon leaned forward in his chair. 'The thing is, it's a bit delicate, we must, how shall I say...proceed slowly - *Siga Siga*. Panos and Eleni nodded.

'Georgios told us about an old house and a plot of land that's for sale. He's been looking out for one for us for a little while. Writing is never going to make me a millionaire and I've got a bank loan to pay off. Anyway, as I was saying, your cousin found us a big property near where we live, overlooking the coast. It's completely run down, it could be renovated by skilled men, like Georgios and his team. The house is owned by a big family and, as you know, it's common for many different family members to own shares in it. It was split between them all, after the old lady who lived there died a few years ago. It's not officially on the market, but Georgios is a man in the know - as you're well aware - and he found out about it quite recently. He's very kindly agreed to negotiate the sale on our behalf, but of course wants to keep his cards close to his chest. So, that's the only reason we're being a bit secretive about all this.' Simon took a long sip of his coffee.

Aisha continued. 'It's not that we didn't want to share our good news with our best friends.'

'It's fine Aisha,' Eleni said, 'We understand perfectly. Simon is correct. You have to be careful here, it's a small island and news travels fast and can be, shall we say, misinterpreted. It can cause bad feelings. Simon, you've been coming here for twenty five years and we value the contribution you've made, coming on holidays, building your house, giving people work, and writing lovely articles about us. You're right to be cautious, there are still some people on the island who are stuck in the past and resent people, who are not from here, making progress. The people who know you will wish you well, as we do of course.' She lifted her coffee up and toasted the couple.

'Good luck to our friends,' Panos said, smiling.

'Thanks guys.' We really appreciate that,' Simon replied.

Panos smiled. 'Your secret is of course safe with us. We shall await news. Of course I won't mention this to Georgios, I'll be the soul of discretion, unless of course he mentions it himself that is.'

Simon smiled. 'Of course mate. Anyway we'll keep in touch and let you know any news, but for the moment we've put our trust in Georgios to deliver,' Simon said.

'Don't worry my friends, my cousin is a master when it comes to these things. You're right to have faith in him.

***

Georgios met up with Simon and Aisha a few weeks later and told them that he'd walked into a *hornet's nest* of thirteen family members for the opening negotiations, all sitting around a huge table. 'A lesser man would have run a mile,' he had joked. He said that it had been quite a hard few hours toing and froing, with so many different family members having their own stubborn point of view. At one point he said that he'd nearly walked away from the deal, as they were being very greedy about the final price and also wanted to keep the olive trees or sell them as a separate purchase. This wasn't unknown in the smaller islands, but he had stuck out for the best deal, which included the olive trees. Eventually they had all managed to come to an agreement, and settled on €50,000, which everyone thought was a fair price. The couple were delighted and couldn't thank Panos's cousin enough. His motives were not altogether altruistic though, as he was making a healthy profit from it too of course, with all the renovations, but everyone was happy.

21

EXCITING PLANS

Georgios had assured them that the work on the retreat would start around the middle of January. This was unusual, as most businesses on the island usually took a few months off after the demands of the tourist season. Georgios said that this would be a favour to the couple, in order to get the retreat ready to open for the Summer season.

'I'm looking forward to Christmas at Grant and Judes,' Aisha said, stretching her legs out on the sofa.

'Yes me too. I know you've only met them a couple of times, but it'll give you a chance to get to know them better. Grant's such a wit and Jude's a fantastic cook. They're both great company.'

Aisha got up and sat at the dining table, and shuffled through some papers.

'Just going off at a slight tangent. We really need to put some sort of business plan together, about the retreat. I've put some preliminary costings together. Would you mind if we talked about it?'

'Of course not - I'd love to. Let's have a look.'

Simon examined the figures that Aisha had prepared. Accounting had never been his strong point but it looked simple enough. Aisha sat down on the couch again and took a sip of her coffee.

'I hate to ask such a personal question - but what are you going to do about your bank loan - you mentioned that you'd paid some off?' asked Aisha.

'Well...I was going to discuss that with you. I'm not able to pay it all off at the moment. As you know I made some money from articles I've written, but that didn't bring a huge amount in. I feel a bit embarrassed actually.'

'Let me help you - so we can start afresh. I'd like to.'

Simon shook his head. 'No way darling. I'm not having you pay off *my* loan. You have enough to do with your money. I'll manage…somehow.'

'But I want to,' Aisha pleaded. 'I have enough. Besides, I've been living off your kindness for nearly a year now. You put a roof over my head and paid for nearly everything. My wages from the taverna have hardly contributed much. Please let me do it, I want to.'

Simon sighed, and got up and walked over to the dining table, and put his arms around her and kissed her. 'Stubborn pride I guess. That's so kind of you. If you're really sure. It's been worrying me, I have to say, but only if you're sure.'

'I'm one hundred percent sure. So that's it sorted. Fresh start - for both of us. Let's go into town to celebrate.'

***

They sat at a table at Mario's cafe. He was open all year round, most of the other cafes and restaurants had closed for the season. The weather was still mild and the sun shone, dappling the tables.

Aisha stretched her legs out and yawned. 'This is the life - so much to look forward to next year.'

Simon lifted his coffee cup. 'Certainly is. I'll drink to that. Any more ideas about what kind of stuff you're going to provide at the retreat.'

Aisha paused for a moment. 'Well, definitely yoga of course, pilates too and some self development stuff, nothing too heavy though. I'll need to find some good tutors, oh and some outdoor stuff, walking holidays, canoeing. I must get in touch with Manos and Maria, the young couple who own the camping shop.'

'It all sounds great. I wouldn't mind leading some of the walks. I never got you lost on Mount Ariadne did I?' he said, grinning.

'That's true. I think you'd be great, but we'd have to get you on a proper walk leader's course, health and safety and all that.'

'Of course. And how about me teaching a creative writing course. I'd love that.'

'Great idea. There you go, we have a draft programme already,' Aisha replied smiling and taking a sip of her coffee. 'We'll need to think about marketing and promotion and stuff too…oh and a website. There's a bit more to this than I thought.'

'One step at a time, we haven't even built the retreat yet.' Simon said.

'Oh and what about a name? What are we going to call it?' Aisha asked.

Simon took another long sip of his coffee and smiled at her. 'It's obvious isn't it?'

'Obvious, not to me?' she replied.

'Remember when I asked you to think of a name for my house last year?'

'Of course.'

'And what did you come up with?'

'The house in the olive grove.'

'Of course - and our new place *Is* an old olive grove. I know it's not the most original, but it's better than calling it some daft hippy name like Moonstone Retreat, or The Lotus Flower.'

'That sounds like a Chinese restaurant.' she laughed.

'Keep it simple. The Olive Grove,' Simon said. Let's stick with that.'

'To the Olive Grove.' Simon lifted his coffee cup.

'To the Olive Grove,' she replied, smiling.

22
CHRISTMAS WITH FRIENDS

It was mid morning on Christmas Day and Simon and Aisha were sitting in Grant and Jude's spacious gardens, soaking up the late December sun. Jude bustled about serving tasty snacks, while keeping an eye on the turkey and serving teas and coffees.

'It's so lovely to meet you again,' Jude said, sitting down beside Aisha - especially after the drama of the fires. It was a terrible time, thank God no one was killed or injured badly. Sven and Mags said that Sven's village is making progress with the rebuilding. He's moved in with her, you may have heard?'

'Yes we had, you know what it's like on this island. They're a real pair of characters, well suited,' Simon replied. 'I'm happy for them.'

'Yes we are too, it's so lovely to see people happy and that includes you two. It's great to be able to sit down and get to know you better Aisha. Simon told us about what you've been through. How have you coped with it all my dear?' Jude asked, placing her hand over Aishas.

'Thank you Jude - you are kind. I don't know. It's been difficult, but we all go through hard times in life - and we're much more resilient than we think. And of course this man here has helped.' She smiled and put her hand on Simon's arm.

Simon smiled back. 'It works both ways, you've been great for me too.' He took a sip of his coffee and leaned back in his chair, enjoying the warmth of the sun on his back.

'It's not all about me though - your lovely Siobhan died - and I've no idea how you must still be feeling. It must be difficult. You keep things to yourself. I can never replace her of course - and would never even try, but I just wanted to say that.'

Simon sighed. 'Of course - I miss her terribly and sometimes - if I'm honest - I feel a bit guilty, that I've found happiness again - so soon. I know she'd have wanted me to be happy. You and her would have liked each other - been friends, I'm sure of it.'

'Simon's right,' Jude said. 'You and dear Siobhan would have got on so well. She was a warm and generous person - just like *you*.'

'Thank you Jude - that means a lot to me,' Aisha replied.

'Thanks for putting us up tonight by the way - it means we can have a drink without worrying about getting a taxi,' Simon said.

'No bother old chap, taxis cost a bloody fortune at Christmas, even though the Greeks don't celebrate it as much as we do - they know there's a fair few of us expats on the island who like a drink and need a taxi home.'

'You have a lovely place here and such beautiful views,' Aisha said.

'I must admit we were very lucky, when we moved here it was just a dilapidated old cottage. It cost a small fortune to renovate and sort all the gardens out mind you. We're thinking of building a small holiday cottage - to supplement our pensons. I can't believe where that time's gone. We were just youngsters back then. I'll be seventy - five soon,' Grant said.

'Time can be a thief all right, Grant. I'll be sixty in a few years. Can't believe it mate,' Simon replied.

'Just a bloody youngster man,' Grant replied, with a broad smile.

Aisha put her hand on her heart. 'You are both young men, in here. Is that not right Jude?'

'Of course - we're all young at heart. Too much is made of people's ages,' Jude replied. 'It's like Grant said, we're so fortunate to live in such a beautiful place - and we have our health of course. Who knows what tomorrow may bring. Live for the moment I say...now...Aisha, would you like to take a little tour of our garden before lunch and see some of our work? I'm into pottery and Grant does watercolours - nothing special but we make a few euros from the tourists in the summer. Simon's seen it all before and we don't want to bore him again.'

'I'd love to.' Aisha replied. I love art and creative people.'

Jude continued. 'We're both ex - art teachers, that's where we met - at art school - in London - the swinging sixties and all that. Follow me my dear.'

Jude led Aisha down the garden to a large blue shed. They went inside.

'How exciting to have lived through that time,' Aisha said.

'Yes it was a bit crazy,' Jude replied. You'd never know it to look at us two wrinklies now though.'

'This is where it all happens,' Jude said, as she opened the door to the shed. 'After you Aisha.'

'Wow! It's like an aladdin's cave.'

'It is a bit I suppose, we've just sort of collected so much stuff over the years.'

Jude's pottery kiln dominated the room and there were dozens of colourful pieces of different sized designs scattered about.

Aisha picked up a small blue and yellow painted vase and turned it over in her hands admiringly.

'I love this, the colours, the texture, it's beautiful.'

'Have it,' said Jude, smiling. 'A gift from me to you.'

'I couldn't,' said Aisha. 'Let me give you something for it.'

'I won't hear of it,' said Jude. 'Merry Christmas.'

Aisha gave Judy a big hug. 'Thank you so much - I know just where this is going in our house and Merry Christmas to you too.'

They moved to the other end of the long shed. 'This is Grant's little studio. It keeps us separated, we'd strangle each other if we didn't have our own space.'

'You're both so talented. I love these seascapes.'

'Grant specialises in them - he sells quite a few in the summer.'

Aisha hesitated as they were getting ready to go out the door. '...I was wondering if we could discuss something, Jude. Simon and I were going to mention it over dinner, but now's as good a time as any I guess.'

'Of course, have a seat darling.' Jude pulled over two small wooden chairs.

'Simon and I are planning a new venture, we're really excited about it... we're going to build a retreat, yoga, self development, walking holidays, stuff like that. We're renovating an old house near us... we're so excited.'

Jude clapped her hands together and gave Aisha a huge warm smile. 'That's absolutely fantastic my dear, what an adventure.'

'Yes, we can't wait to get it completed and open up in the Summer, hopefully, fingers crossed...I was wondering...if you and Grant, with your backgrounds, your creativity, if you'd be interested in running some courses for us, you're both so talented. I'm sure people would love to learn pottery and painting.'

Jude swept her grey hair back from her face...'Well, you've certainly thrown in a Christmas Day surprise there my girl. I'm not sure what to say. Firstly...thank you of course, I'm flattered and Grant will be too, but aren't we a bit old for this sort of thing? I mean it's been years since we both taught. I'll certainly give it some consideration, but I think the problem's going to be that we'd need a load more potter's wheels and a bigger kiln of course. If I was going to teach. It was a lovely offer though.' Jude said, trying to let Aisha down gently.

'I never thought of that,' said Aisha, sounding a bit crestfallen. 'How silly of me. There's more to this than I realised obviously. It's my impetuous side.'

Jude patted Aisha on the knee. 'Impetuous is good - it brings creativity... don't give yourself a hard time my dear. I can't speak for Grant, but in theory, it'd be much easier for him to teach watercolours - there would be far less equipment needed. Let's go back and have a chat with him about it.'

Aisha paused in the doorway. 'Of course. We're just putting a draft programme together and a website, and all the promotional stuff.'

'Sounds exhausting. Grant may be able to help you with the website, he's really good at IT stuff - when he's sober that is.' Judy let out a small sigh. 'Now Let's go and see what those boys are up to.'

Jude and Aisha arrived back at the table. Grant and Simon had opened a bottle of white wine and were chatting animatedly. 'Well look who's back, thought you'd been kidnapped by aliens, girls,' Grant said.

'Yes, we were just saying, who's going to cook Christmas dinner now if you two didn't come back?' Simon replied.

'Sexist rubbish,' Aisha replied. smiling. I know that you can cook, and I'm sure Grant can too. Is that all you want us for,' she smiled.

'Ha, of course not ladies, we're just joshing. Glass of wine?' Grant enquired.

'Bit early, even for me,' said Jude...'Go on then.'

'I'll have one too please,' said Aisha. It's Christmas after all.'

'What's that you've got,' Simon asked.

'It's a wonderful Christmas present, from Jude, she's so kind. It's beautiful, don't you think.' She set the vase down on the table beside Simon, and she and Jude sat down, as Grant poured them some wine.

Simon picked up the vase and rolled it over in his large hands and held it up to the light. 'It's a cracker. What talented friends we have 'He put it back down and reached for his glass. 'Here's to talented friends.'

'To talented friends,' they chorused.

'Now... what's all this stuff about a retreat?' Grant enquired. 'This man here's been telling me that you have great plans Aisha.

'Yes, well we were going to leave it 'till later to tell you our news, but I blurted it out to Jude in the studio. Seems like neither of us can keep a...'

'It's fantastic news darling isn't it,' Jude gently interrupted. 'How exciting for our little island. And they want *You* to teach watercolour courses.'

'I know old girl. Simon asked me earlier. I shall give it serious consideration I can assure you. I'm very touched that you think an old bugger like me can still come up with the goods.'

'I've seen your paintings, Grant, they're amazing. We'd love you to join us in our dream. Even if you just started off in a small way, that would be great,' Aisha said, touching Grant's hand.

'I have heard that painting holidays are very popular now,' Grant said - warming to the subject. 'Might keep me off the gin too.' he smiled at Jude. 'And anyhow, who could refuse such a gorgeous girl.'

Aisha lent over and hugged Grant. 'Oh Grant thank you so much, you are officially our first tutor at the Olive Grove Retreat.'

'I'm very honoured indeed.' Grant smiled and drank the rest of his wine.

23

THE RETREAT

Work on the retreat had been stop - start, due to some stormy Winter weather, but now they were into early April - the sun shone most days and the temperature was rising. Georgios had reassured them that he could meet the new deadline of early June. They had managed to save most of the structure of the old cottage and the new extension had been sympathetically designed to fit in. The twenty rooms were nearly complete and the small swimming pool was almost finished. The islanders who had been hibernating or travelling abroad to see friends, gradually emerged. The shopkeepers and bar and restaurant owners began to start working on their businesses in preparation for the season ahead. This year Simon and Aisha would be joining them. They were sitting in their garden, enjoying a coffee in the sunshine and had their laptop and paperwork set out on the table.

'It's been a hectic few months but Georgios has come good,' said Simon.

'Yes, he and his men are making a fantastic job of it. He reckons the pool will be up and working in the next few weeks,' Aisha replied.

'Fantastic.' Simon took a sip of his coffee

'How's the bookings going?'

Aisha shuffled some spreadsheets. 'Really good, a bit slow to start with - but Grant's made such a great job of the website - it should pick up soon - especially when we're able to post proper photos in a few weeks, instead of the virtual ones.'

'That's great. Did you get all the licences from the Mayor?' he asked

'All sorted - apart that is from the main one - our tourism operating license - without that we can't open. But... Yannis said he would try and bring that along on the opening night and present it to us - put on a bit of a show,' she replied, pulling some papers out from the pile.

'Try? Simon had panic in his voice. 'That doesn't sound very positive darling. Sorry, I didn't mean to overreact or doubt you there. Bloody paperwork's a nightmare in Greece. I've known Yannis for years, - and I know he'll try and speed things up for us... If you can use the word *speed* in Greece that is.'

'Yes I'm beginning to learn that - it's not so unlike Bosnia in some respects.'

'Can you bring up that spreadsheet with all the courses and the leaders' names on it please darling,' he asked.

'Sure,' Aisha replied, scrolling down to find it. They both peered at the screen, the sunlight obscured their view a little.

'Ok, so I'm doing the opening yoga and meditation week. Grant's doing the watercolour painting week. Did Sven get back to you about doing the Reiki course?' Aisha enquired.

'Not yet, I'll chase him up. Lovely guy but so laid back he's almost horizontal,' Grant replied. 'I guess that helps if you're a therapist though. Other courses?' he asked.

'Dimitri and Maria in the camping shop have still to confirm about doing the sea kayaking week. Did you say you had a friend who does driftwood art?' she asked.

'Yes, Sophie, you've not met her yet.'

'No but we need to contact her - see if she's willing to put on a course. I want to get as much stuff in the diary as possible for the next few months.'

'I've texted her a few times, but no reply, I think she has a new love interest - so she might be busy.' He smiled as he pulled out his phone from his pocket. 'I'll text her again now.'

'What about *your* creative writing course? Have you decided about it?'

'Yes, I'm going to do it, I've never taught before but I'll learn I guess.'

'Of course you will - you're a fantastic writer and you can inspire people. You'll be fine.'

'Ok, that's potentially six weeks of courses. What's next on the agenda?' Simon asked.

Aisha drank the last of her coffee and picked up her To Do list... 'Let me see. We need to get Georgios men to finish landscaping the gardens - the pool's nearly done - check the beds and bedding and the furniture for the rooms are going to be delivered on time. We have to interview a head chef and two kitchen staff - and they'll need to have up to date food hygiene certificates. I already mentioned the photos for the website. Grant's onto that though. - and last but not least - we'll have to find cleaners and a gardener too - easy!' she giggled.

Simon's brow furrowed. 'Bloody hell. I never thought there was so much to it to be honest. *I* can do the gardens - for the first few weeks anyway... we'll save money too. Talking of which - how's the budget doing?'

'Tight. We might not need *all* of those people at first of course - but we're better planning to be busy - otherwise what's the point of opening a business?' Aisha said.

'You're right and it's so exciting too. What an adventure eh?'

She leaned over and touched his arm and smiled. 'I'm glad you're feeling more positive. We'll be fine.'

***

There were four weeks to go before the official opening and Simon and Aisha and Panos and Eleni were up at the retreat for a visit. Parts of it still looked like a building site, but overall they were very pleased with progress.

Panos was talking to Georgios. 'You and the men have done a great job, cousin. It looks fantastic and you managed to keep all the gardens and the olive groves.'

'Yes that was a bit tricky mate, as we had to alter the shape of some of the buildings, but we managed it,' Georgios replied.

'We're really pleased with it, Georgios,' Simon said, putting his arm around Aisha.'

'Yes - thanks so much. Did you say you were hoping to finish in three weeks?' Aisha asked, nervously.

'Give or take a few days, yes.' He pointed over at a large pile of rubble and old bricks. 'All of this rubbish will be cleared up by then I promise. I know it looks a bit of an eyesore, but we'll soon have it looking pretty.'

'It's fantastic, Eleni said. 'Can we have a look inside. Is it safe?'

'Of course - follow me,' said Georgios.

He took them on a tour of the fifteen rooms, they were simply but beautifully furnished, as was the staff apartment, the kitchen, dining room, meditation rooms, library and outdoor spaces. There was a small bar near the pool and an indoor one too.

'When's the opening party?' Panos asked.

'Funny you should say that mate. We were just thinking the same thing. Hopefully two weeks before the actual date guests arrive. If things go to plan - in four weeks time. That reminds me - you kindly said you can help us stock the bar - when it's finally completed. I know you've got the taverna to get ready for the season, but I'd appreciate it mate,' Simon said.

'My pleasure my friend,' Panos replied.

Eleni touched Aisha's shoulder. 'Oh while I remember Aisha, I think I've found you a head chef - Dimitroula, my sister's daughter. She's young, not long finished catering college, but she's won lots of awards and is a very hard worker. I'll ask her to contact you this week if that's ok?'

'That's wonderful Eleni, thank you.' Aisha reached over to give Eleni a big hug.

'Oh and I've managed to contact two ladies who'll help out in the kitchen too, - and I think I've also found you a couple of reliable cleaners,' Eleni added.

'This is fantastic! Thanks so much Eleni - you've taken so much stress off me.' Aisha said.

'It's my pleasure. I know how difficult it is to find good, reliable staff.'

'Yes- thanks so much Eleni. My head's spinning with it all,' Simon said.

Eleni laughed. 'You'll soon get used to the pressure. You should try running a taverna, eh my love,' she said, looking at Panos.

'Oh yes my dear, not as easy as it looks, but we have years of experience. You two are mere novices.' he grinned.

'We appreciate all the help we can get,' Aisha said, as the little tour ended back beside the pool.

***

The opening night party finally arrived. Simon and Aisha were feeling a little nervous, and Aisha flitted about finishing this and tidying that. Aisha had found some colourful bunting in town and she and Jude had strung it along the bar and pool area. It looked bright and vivid in the strong May sunshine. There were some snags still to fix before the guests were due to arrive in a few weeks, but it was all going pretty smoothly. Simon and Aisha had invited their close friends, the builders and their families, Manos and Maria from the camping shop and the new staff members and some local dignitaries, including the Mayor, Yannis. He was an important person and had to be schmoozed. He hadn't yet signed off the final building work, so they could get the all important tourism operating license - to begin trading. Simon was trying to keep his nerves steady about that - and he'd left that to Aisha and her womanly wiles to work her magic.

It was a hot and humid early May evening and a throng of people were gathered around the pool area, which had all been beautifully finished and the azure water sparkled in the early evening sun. There was a wonderful exciting energy in the air and the hum of convivial conversation. They'd hired a catering company, to take some pressure off themselves.

Sophie had finally been found and Simon introduced her to Aisha.

'Lovely to meet you,' said Aisha, who was wearing a stunning blue silk dress, which showed off her fabulous figure. 'Simon tells me that you've kindly agreed to run a course for us, driftwood sculpture - yes?'

'Yes that's right. I'm so looking forward to it. It's lovely to meet you too.' She brushed back her blond hair from her face with her hand and looked towards a tall, tanned man in his mid thirties who was standing beside her. He was wearing a white linen jacket and slacks. This is Giovanni.'

'Nice to meet you.' Aisha offered her hand.

'Lovely to meet you Aisha,' he replied.

Simon looked on with a tinge of butterflies in his stomach, as the guests gathered in busy groups, clinking glasses and enjoying the canapes. The old gang were all there. Sven and Mags, Grant and Jude, Sophie and her new boyfriend, Georgios and his men and their families - their new head chef Dimitroula and the rest of the catering and cleaning staff, and their families and of course - their best friends Panos and Eleni. They'd even found Alfred, from the forest fires adventure and he was there with his partner. Roula and Dimitrii were having a fine time, chasing their cousin Georgio's kids around the newly landscaped gardens and pool area. Simon spotted some new guests arriving and recognised Yannis the Mayor and his wife and also the chief of police and chief fire commissioner and their wives. He had thought it prudent to invite them - after the forest fires incident. He took hold of Aisha's hand and propelled her towards them.

'Excuse us for a minute folks, the Mayor's arrived,' he shouted over his shoulder.

Good evening Mr Mayor, Chief of police and Chief Fire Commissioner. Thanks so much for coming,' Simon said. 'You've met Aisha of course,' he said, shaking the Mayor's hand.

'Of course- a pleasure to see you again my dear,' the Mayor said, shaking Aisha's hand. Simon noticed that the two middle aged men both stole discreet, approving glances at Aisha, while they were waiting to be greeted.

Simon and Aisha shook the hands of the Chief of Police and the Chief Fire Commissioner.

'Please follow us gentleman and we'll get you a drink,' Aisha said, beckoning the three men and their wives towards her.

Simon smiled. *Got them eating out of her hand* he thought . *This is going to be a great night.*

After about an hour and several drinks Simon nodded to Aisha. He decided it was time. He and Aisha walked to a space by the side of the pool in front of their guests. He took out a large piece of paper on which he'd written a pre-prepared speech. It all went quiet.

He straightened his white linen jacket and looked and smiled at Aisha, who stood next to him. She smiled and rubbed his back reassuringly.

He gave a nervous cough. 'Ahem - I was going to read this speech but I don't want to bore you all and there's eating and drinking to be done.' A ripple of laughter went around, as he ripped up the paper and put it back in his pocket. More laughter followed.

'Ladies and gentlemen, children, friends, our builders, new work colleagues and esteemed dignitaries... I can't tell you how much pleasure it gives Aisha and myself - to see The Olive Grove Retreat completed, in such a beautiful fashion, by Georgios and his wonderful builders. *Efahristo poli Georgios.*' Simon raised his glass. Giorgos and his men smiled, gave a little bow and raised their glasses, as everyone gave them a huge round of applause.

'Enough from me.' He pulled Aisha close to him. 'This beautiful lady here is the brains behind all this and it's her dream and her baby.'

Aisha took a little time to look over at everyone and smiled... 'Thank you darling... I feel emotional tonight. Not only have you all welcomed me to your beautiful island and into your lovely community - but you have welcomed me into your hearts... a ripple of applause ran around the pool area. You have all... in your different ways, helped me - I should say - *us*, achieve our dream, and it has come true tonight. I want to take a minute to say a very special thank you to our dear friends Panos and Eleni. Simon has known you both for many years, when you befriended him and his dear wife Siobhan.' Simon took out a handkerchief from his pocket and dabbed his eyes... 'You have both been fantastic friends to me too. We would never have achieved half of this without your friendship, love - and generosity. Thank you so much.' Panos and Eleni had beaming smiles on their faces, and raised their glasses, to huge applause.

Aisha dabbed her eyes with a tissue and continued. 'Never...in a million years did I think that when I found myself here by accident, on Xanthos over a year ago, that I would be standing here tonight and with so many lovely new friends and in such beautiful surroundings. I want to thank you all so much, from here.' She touched her heart - and waited until the unrestrained applause had died down and took Simon's hand and faced him.

'But...I could not have done any of this without this lovely man...who has quite simply changed my life...He helped me when I was down... and cheered me up with his crazy Irish humour. He looked after me... when I needed a friend and introduced me to all of you lovely people.... I love him so much.'

Aisha wiped a tear from her eyes, as Simon hugged her. This was followed by more thunderous applause - as people put down their glasses and clapped and whooped, as Simon and Aisha held one another.

Panos and Eleni came over with a huge bottle of champagne and a massive bouquet of flowers for the couple. The cheering and applause took a while to die down.

Simon spotted the tall slim figure of Yannis the Mayor pushing through the crowd towards them.

He arrived at the little group, and gave Simon and Aisha another firm handshake.' Would you mind calling for a bit of silence please Simon?'

'Of course Mr Mayor.' Simon banged a fork on the side of his wine glass a few times until the crowd reluctantly quietened down.

'Can I please have silence for our Mayor, thank you.'

Mayor Yannis straightened up his tall frame and spoke slowly and deliberately...

'Ladies and gentlemen. It is my great pleasure for my wife and I... to be invited here tonight... for the opening of Aisha and Simon's new retreat - The Olive Grove. I know they will make a great success of it...I have known Simon for many years, since he began coming to Xanthos and I have always found him to be a very warm, friendly and pleasant and sincere man, who loves our little piece of paradise in the Aegean...and that is why he keeps coming back here year after year... I believe that he is also a bit of a connoisseur... of our local wines and brandies.' Much loud laughter and applause followed. Simon and Aisha had huge grins on their faces and Panos gave the Mayor the thumbs up sign... The Mayor waited until it had quietened down a bit...'The Olive Grove Retreat will provide much needed jobs for local people - on our small island - as well as giving a boost to our tourist trade - and keeping us on the map... I wish you both every success in the future.' He held a blue official looking folder up in his right hand. 'And now, it only remains for me to present the final tourism operating licence of approval. Good luck - or Kali Tychi as we say here in Greece.'

Simon gave Aisha a gentle push forward and she accepted the folder from the Mayor and shook his hand. Simon did likewise. More rowdy applause followed.

'Thank you Mr Mayor!' Simon shouted above the din. 'Thank you!'

24
OPENING DAY

The day has finally arrived. Aisha wrote in the brand new shiny visitor's book. *Saturday 8th June 2019 - The Olive Grove is Open* and she added a big smiley face. Simon was bustling about the dining room, the birds were singing and the sun shone into the room like a torch beam, illuminating the new paintwork.

'Slow down, the ferry is not due until midday, you're like a cat on hot bricks, it's only 9am,' Aisha said.

'Can't find that bloody list of guests you gave me earlier,' Simon replied, looking flustered.

'Here it is darling.' She passed him a folder. 'I don't think I've ever seen you so nervous. Now sit down and have a coffee, it's all under control.'

'Thought I'd lost it. I haven't had a look at the updated list since last week.'

'I have. Someone's booked at the last minute - a Father Seamus Kelly,' Aisha said.

'Father, a priest? Unusual... I used to know a Seamus Kelly. We were friends growing up in Belfast - it's not an unusual name in Northern Ireland though. He certainly wasn't priest material - I can assure you. A wee rogue so he was.'

'I love it when you speak in your Belfast accent when you're nervous.' Aisha smiled 'I suppose priests need holidays too - they have a tough job - looking after everyone else.'

'Yes of course - you just never think of priests having holidays.'

Simon finally sat down and she handed him the guest list. 'That's fifteen guests, full up - not bad for our opening week.

'Oh, have you checked with Michaelis about the coach coming here first to pick you up?' she asked.

He laid his hand on hers. 'Now who's panicking, relax, I phoned him first thing. He's picking me up at eleven..'

Aisha smiled and kissed his head. 'Good - It's going to be a beautiful day.'

***

Simon stood at the top of the jetty with a clipboard and a big cardboard sign saying THE OLIVE GROVE. Aisha had painted a bunch of garish black and green olives on it. Several of the guests had found him - and stood in front of him with their suitcases, looking at him expectantly. 'Good morning everyone and welcome to Xanthos, and to the Olive Grove Retreat! Please give me your name!' Simon said loudly, so he could be heard among the bustle of the port. He gave out his best big smile, as the throng of tourists swept past him. 'When I've taken your name, can you please get on the small mini-bus behind me - Michaelis our lovely driver will sort your luggage - thanks everyone.' Several more people approached him - most of them looked a little apprehensive. After a few minutes, Simon had begun to pick out the ones that had that look about them, and had guessed that most of them were coming to the retreat.

'Just one more guest and we'll be on our way Michaelis,' Simon said, looking at his clipboard and scanning the crowds.

Michaelis nodded patiently.

A tall, stocky, middle aged - balding figure came up to him, smiling - and set his suitcase down. 'Hello my friend - it's been a wee while.' He had a strong Belfast accent.

Simon frowned and scrutinised the man's rather battered face. 'Sorry - you have me there sir. I recognise the accent of course. Have we met?' Simon replied.

'That we have my man. It's *me* Simon...Seamus, Seamus Kelly... I recognised you from your photo on the website. It's been nearly forty years, so I don't blame you for not recognising *me*. And the hair's gone too - as you see,' he said, smiling and touching his bald head.

'What the feck!...Seamus...of course. I recognise you now,' he said, as he hugged his old friend - he lapsed into his old lingo. 'This is feckin surreal - and yer a priest for feck sake.'

Michaelis looked on with bemused bewilderment.

***

The mini - bus came to a halt at the retreat twenty five minutes later. There were murmurs of appreciation for the brand new sign - consisting of colourful mosaics - saying: The Olive Grove.' It was tastefully designed with silver olive leaves and black olives.

Simon picked up the microphone and flicked it on. 'Welcome to The Olive Grove everyone, don't worry about your luggage. Michaelis will bring it inside for you. Please mind your step as you get off.

He could see Aisha and the new chef Dimitroula and her helpers, Maria and Katerina, standing, smiling, with trays of sparkling wine, waiting for their guests. The excited and wide -eyed guests followed Simon through the newly built archway and into the outside patio dining area.

'Welcome - Welcome,' Aisha repeated, with a dazzling smile - as she and the other two women handed out the wine to the delighted guests.

The new arrivals sat on the patio on white plastic chairs, the air was buzzing with conversations of newly found friends and the first day of holidays excitement. The fifteen guests were a mixture, with the women outnumbering the three men, and Aisha guessed that they were in their late thirties, up to late fifties. Everyone began to settle and enjoy their wine in the blazing sunshine, while Dimitroula and Maria went round topping up their glasses. Aisha had thoughtfully placed small bowls of nuts and olives on the tables. Simon stepped forward and Aisha stood beside him. He gestured over to her.

'Hi everyone. You know I'm Simon - and this is my partner Aisha and she's going to say a few words.'

Aisha cleared her throat a little nervously, then gave out a huge beaming smile. 'Thanks Simon. Welcome everyone. Welcome to the Olive Grove Retreat...*YOU* are our very first guests and we are *so* happy and excited to have you here.' She glanced down at her notes.

'I'll be your tutor for your Yoga and Meditation week. More about that later. First...some practicalities. Simon and I will be staying on-site this week, so we are available day and night... Hopefully just day.' A ripple of laughter echoed round the patio.

'We're here to look after you, so we want you to relax from the minute you walked through our gates. We know you'll be tired from travelling so we won't overload you... Now... before I tell you any more, as it's getting near lunchtime, a very important subject...food.' A ripple of laughter followed. She gestured over to Dimitroula and her two staff, who stood side by side near her. 'This is Dimitroula, our head chef, and the lovely ladies beside her are Maria and Katerina.' The three women all smiled self consciously. 'They'll be cooking delicious meals for you during your week here. If you have any special diets or allergies you haven't told us about, please let us know as soon as you can, so we can make sure you enjoy our wonderful food. You will see that there are some small fridges scattered about the Olive Grove, with free water, milk and fruit juices and also tea and coffee making facilities. The times of your meals are on the back of your room doors. Lunch today will be served at 12:30. It's 11.30 now, so not long to wait. You don't have to remember all this, it's all on the information boards. We will take you on a short tour soon and show you your rooms.

Simon took the microphone. 'Thank you Aisha. Talking of another... very important subject - alcohol - I'm in charge of the bar.' A small cheer went up and he smiled. 'I thought you'd like that. We'll be opening at one o'clock... or earlier if you're desperate.' Another ripple of laughter greeted Simon's remark. 'We're also open from 6.30pm 'till late every evening.'

Aisha touched his shoulder and smiled. 'Thank you Simon. Now, if everyone would like to follow us, we'll show you around. Michaelis has left your bags outside.'

Simon and Aisha had shown everyone to their rooms and left them to unpack before lunch. They just had time to draw breath and grab a coffee together on the dining room patio.

'They all seem like lovely people,' Aisha remarked.

'Yes they do - it's going to be a great week - I can feel it,' Simon said. 'Oh I meant to say - and you will not believe me - but that priest - Father Kelly, he *is* the guy I knew from back in Belfast. I'm still in shock.'

'Oh my god -that is amazing. How many years?'

'Nearly forty.' Simon shook his head.

'Lots to catch up on then my darling.'

Dimitroula had cooked a feast. It was laid out buffet style under the heated counter and there was also a huge salad bar and freshly baked bread. There were oohs and aahs from the guests as they came in - and smelt the wonderful aromas. And even more when they spotted the amazing colourful and beautifully presented food. One of the guests was followed in by a small tabby cat.

'Is this your cat?' a young woman asked Aisha?

'I've never seen him - or her before. Perhaps it belongs to one of our neighbours. Doesn't have a collar. It's cute though,' Aisha said, scooping it up and gently putting it back outside on the patio.

The place was buzzing with first day excitement, people were already mingling and having fun and it was clear that they had a good bunch of guests. Dimitroula told Aisha that her and Maria and Katerina were very happy - as the guests had already complimented them on their food. Aisha made sure to thank them.

Simon and Aisha had sat down for lunch with two of the guests, to get to know them better. Mike and Suzie were from London and were both artists, in their late forties Simon guessed.

'This food is amazing,' Suzie said between mouthfuls. 'So fresh and tasty.'

'Thank you Suzie. I will let Dimitroula know. She's very young for a head chef, but she came to us highly recommended. We're very lucky to have her and to also have such amazing fresh produce.'

'It's going to be a great week. You've created something special here,' Mike said, looking around.

'Thank you Mike. It's very much a team effort,' Aisha replied.

Everyone had nearly finished their lunch, when she stood up and tapped a glass with a knife to get people's attention. 'Hi everyone. Sorry to interrupt your lunch. I just wanted to let you know some more bits and pieces. We don't want to overload you with information on your first day though.' She glanced down at her notes on the table and pointed over to the outside bar area. 'Simon will be opening the bar in five minutes.' A cheer went up. 'I thought you'd like that. We'll be having a small get - together this evening before dinner…in the lounge at 6.30, just so that we can all introduce ourselves. I'll also tell you a bit more about the programme for the week. You'll see a copy is also up on the notice board in the Lounge next to the indoor dining room,' she said pointing over. Please take a look at it when you're ready…we also have a Tai Chi session every morning. If you want to start your day in that way - before breakfast, the class is at 8am, for you early birds, in the gardens beside the meditation rooms. I'll go over all this again later. Oh, I nearly forgot, Thursday is market day in Neo Horio, it's a fantastic little market, if you want to buy some souvenirs to take home. And if any of you just want some time to yourself, you can go to the beach or just chill here by the pool. So there will be no Yoga or Meditation on Thursday. Any questions, you can find us in the office where we showed you earlier. Thank you.' Everyone clapped in appreciation.

Simon lifted the metallic shutter causing a squeaking sound, which caught everyone's attention. 'Bar's open everyone! Oh I almost forgot - we don't take cash, so just give us your room number…and not anyone else's mind you - and we'll make a note of what you have and give you your bill on the last day. I hope that's ok with you all, saves mucking about with cash.'

Everyone murmured their approval, and joined the queue at the bar.

'A pint of your best Greek lager please Si,' Seamus said.

'Haven't been called Si since Belfast. Coming up Seamus. I still can't believe you're here, after all these years. Thought I might have seen you back there at some point, but not on a Greek island. We'll hopefully have time to chat later mate - we've a lot to catch up on.'

'That we have Si- cheers!'

Aisha walked over to him, smiling. 'You're in your element here darling.'

Simon smiled back at her. 'Can't argue with that.'

It had turned out to be quite an early night for most of the guests, as Simon had anticipated. When he'd done his meditation week in the Spanish mountains years ago, everyone had tried to stay up late on the first night too. They were on a high and wanted to let go of all the stress that people carry in everyday life, without even realising it and make the most of every minute of holiday freedom. They were tired from travelling and adrenaline - and this eventually caught up with them all, apart from Seamus. He and Simon were desperate to talk and it wasn't quite midnight yet.

Aisha joined them at the bar. 'Simon told me that you two go back a very long way, Seamus,' Asha said.

'We grew up in the same street - and it's been many years since we last saw each other.

'I was telling Aisha, Seamus, that I'd never have picked you out to become a priest, back in the day,' Simon said.

Seamus smiled. 'And you were dead right. I was a bit of a wee rogue back then Aisha, getting into all sorts of scrapes.'

'We haven't had much time to talk today - as we've been so busy - but he also told me - about your poor young brother. Do you mind me mentioning it, Seamus?' Aisha said.

Seamus paused, and took a big gulp of his beer...'Not at all my dear. Gerry was only sixteen when he was killed. He was hit by a bullet from a British soldier. They said it was a tragic mistake - and that he was in the wrong place at the wrong time. He was throwing stones at the soldiers and the police, so maybe he shouldn't have been there. It's what a lot of young lads did on a Friday night I'm afraid. I'm not excusing it, however, the soldier was charged with Gerry's murder, and he went to court, but he got off with it.'

'That must have been a terrible time for your family.'

'It was devastating.'

'Were you around at the time darling?'

No - I'd not long left to go to London - to start my journalist training. I never saw much of Seamus after that. Life just took over. The next thing I heard about you was that you...'

'Went to prison,' Seamus interrupted. 'It's ok Si, it's part of my life - it happened. I wish it hadn't but it did.'

'I'll keep it brief Aisha, as it's late and we all have to be up in the morning. Not long after Gerry died, I got involved in a lot of violence, like many other lads my age. I was burning with anger for the British - or Brits as we called them back then. I got involved in some pretty hairy stuff - and eventually it caught up with me. I was jailed for three years. My wee Mammy was heartbroken.'

'How tough was that.' asked Aisha.

'Very.'

But something good came of it. About two years into my sentence I got talking to the prison priest - and he told me about the training required. He changed my life - otherwise I would have probably come out and started all over again. The guys I was in prison with couldn't believe it - my family couldn't believe it either. And I had trouble believing it myself for a while. Was I taking the easy way out - absolving myself of my sins and all that? I thought long and hard about it all. So...Si was right - it was a huge shock to everyone who knew me. My Mammy and my Da were very happy though. It's quite a feather in your cap to have a priest in the family - in the Catholic community.'

Simon nodded in agreement.

'Anyhow...my friends - it's time this old priest was getting his beauty sleep. We have yoga in the morning. And that's why I came here after all. Well, that's one of the reasons,' he said enigmatically.

Aisha and Simon gave Seamus a hug.

'We'll see you at breakfast,' Simon said.

25

YOGA AND MEDITATION

The opening day had gone well and everyone seemed to get on and they were settling in.

Simon was sipping his coffee on the balcony with Aisha, before the guests arrived for breakfast. He sighed. 'I'm knackered.'

'It was a late night. You needed to catch up with Seamus. You're lucky, you had a long lie this morning. I got up early for Tai Chi.' Aisha playfully slapped his arm.

'Yes it was amazing seeing him again after so long…I suppose I'd better go and have a shave eh. Make myself presentable for our guests.'

'Yes you'd better,' she said. 'You don't want to scare them.'

Aisha was aware of the cat rubbing against her legs under her chair. They'd decided it was a girl and christened it Olive. No one had come forward to claim it yet. She picked it up and gave it a cuddle as it purred loudly.

'You love that cat more than me,' he said

'Only slightly,' she smiled. 'He's so cute.'

'And what about me?'

'You've never been cute…handsome yes, but not cute.'

Simon had finished shaving and showering and prepared some muesli and chopped up bananas. When he'd finished he took his cup of coffee out to the balcony. It was 10am and Aisha would be starting her first Yoga and

Meditations session of the week. He drained the last of his coffee, then heard his phone ping. He had a text from Jude asking him to phone her. He called her number and she answered right away.

'Thanks for getting back to me so quickly darling. Do you have five minutes?'

'Just about - it's pretty hectic here,' Simon replied.

'Of course. I'll be brief.

'It's about Donald Ruthven.'

'What about him?' Simon bristled at the mention of the name.

'I met Jenny in town yesterday. Donald's been diagnosed with incurable lung cancer. He has carers coming in to look after him.'

He could feel the anger rising. 'Am I expected to feel sorry for him Jude - is that it?'

'No of course not - no - he's apparently become very religious.'

'Go on.'

'Well, anyway, Jenny said that he wants to make amends to people he's upset in the past.'

'That's going to take a while then.'

'I know - I was cynical too when she said that.'

'He wants to meet you - to say sorry.'

Simon laughed. '*Me* - Not a hope in hell Jude.'

'I don't blame you for being angry darling. Jenny said that he's genuine about it though - he's been seeing an Anglican priest.'

'I need to go Jude,' Simon cut in. 'We're very busy here, it's the first week and all. I'm sorry if I sound rude - I appreciate that you're only passing a message.'

'Ok darling - love to Aisha - so sorry to keep you - you must both be up to your eyes in it.'

'Bye Jude.'

He sat down and sighed heavily and put his head in his hands. *Fucking unreal - the cheeky bastard.*' he thought to himself. He looked in the mirror and brushed his hair back with his hand and went into the bathroom and threw some water on his face - and dried it with a towel. Then he slowly went down the steps and walked past the pool - to the flat grassy yoga and meditation area. Aisha was doing some stretches before her class started.

'Sorry to interrupt. Just thought I'd come down and wish you well, your first class and all that. I wasn't going to tell you 'til later, but you won't believe what Jude's just told me.'

'Jude?' Aisha replied, looking puzzled.

'She sent me a text earlier- asking me to get in touch with her.'

'What about?'

Ruthven has cancer - it's incurable and he wants to meet people he's upset in the past - and apologise to them - including me - he's gone all religious apparently. It's crazy - fucking crazy.'

Aisha shook her head. 'The ex- major you had a fight with?'

'Yes - I know you've never met him. Anyway I told her, it's not happening - *ever*.'

'I don't blame you darling - we can talk about it later if you want.'

'No it's fine. I'm sorry to disturb you. I know this is a big moment. I just wanted to wish you well.'

He gave her a huge hug.

'Thank you. I feel great. I have to keep pinching myself. I'd better get ready, they'll be here soon. What's your schedule today?'

'I'm going to trim back some of the bushes and then clean the pool - and then have a break and help out in the kitchen, if they'll have me.' he smiled.

'Sounds great,' Aisha replied.

He blew her a kiss. 'Good luck. See you at lunch.

He made his way down to the shed where he kept all the gardening stuff, and pulled out a small tree saw and lifted the wheelbarrow and walked over beside the pool. The heat was rising and his t-shirt clung to his back. There were some delicious aromas coming from the kitchen area. It was 10.30am. Aisha would be well into her class by now. He walked quietly over to the outdoor Yoga and Meditation area. A huge stone statue of a sitting Buddha dominated the garden. Aisha was taking the guests through some positions and he thought that she really looked the part. He spotted Seamus, who gave him a discreet wave.

After a break for lunch, Aisha finished her Meditation class around 3pm and left her guests to themselves, some jumped in the pool to cool off - and others went back to their rooms for a siesta. She and Simon had been too busy to meet up for lunch. Aisha walked in the door. Simon was sitting on the balcony enjoying a coffee and she came over and kissed him on the head.

'Alright for some.' she smiled.

'Yeah, easy life. I've just this minute finished gardening, honest…How did it go? You look happy - coffee?'

'Yes please.'

He padded barefoot into the kitchen and switched the kettle on.

'It was fantastic. I'm buzzing, it went far better than I thought it would.'

'I told you that you'd no need to be nervous. I knew you'd smash it. That's my girl - I'm so proud of you.' He came out of the kitchen and put his arm around her, she smelt of sweat and sun tan cream.

'Thanks, they're a lovely bunch too - so warm and friendly.'

'That's wonderful, you must be tired though.'

'I am and it's only the second day,' she sighed - throwing herself down on the couch.

'It's so hot too, I'll pace myself better tomorrow, now that I've got a better idea of everyone's capabilities.'

'Of course you will.' Simon came into the lounge and passed her a coffee.

'Ahh thanks, I've been needing this.' She took a sip, and wrapped her fingers around the warm mug, and kicked off her sandals and stretched her legs out.

'You sure you don't want to talk about this Ruthven thing, darling?'

'Absolutely positive - but thanks - I still can't believe the cheek of the bastard.'

***

The bar had quietened down a bit after the initial evening rush.

Seamus took a sip of his brandy. 'I know that you and Aisha are incredibly busy - and that I've just landed here in front of you after all these years - I know it's a lot to ask, but … can I confide in you Si?

'Of course - we're old friends,' Simon replied.

'This is going to sound a bit mad. I came here for the retreat of course… but that was a secondary reason. I alluded to it last night… I got a strange email a couple of weeks ago… from someone asking to meet me - he's connected with my past and Gerry's death. He's an ex-army officer…I can't believe I'm going to say this, but… he's the soldier that shot our Gerry… and he lives right here…on this island. I know it sounds like a film or something… but it's true.'

Simon's eyes widened…'His name's not Ruthven is it?'

Seamus looked shocked…. 'Yes…how the hell did you know that?'

It's a tiny island mate,' and we only have *one* ex-British Army officer - as far as I know,' Simon replied.

Seamus continued. 'Of course - I'm not thinking straight. I didn't realise how small your community is - I nearly said Parish... He was a young officer in Belfast when it happened. They put him on trial for Gerry's death - but he was found not guilty - they said it was *an accident* - as I alluded to last night...I always reckoned it was a cover up though. Those were dark days back then - as you well know.

Simon was listening intently. 'I remember hearing about it and seeing it on the news when I lived in London. It shocked me to the core about wee Gerry.'

Seamus took out a piece of folded paper from his pocket and handed it over to Simon, who carefully opened the printed email and smoothed it out on the bar top, before picking up his glasses.

Dear Father Kelly.

I have no doubt that you will be shocked and upset to receive this email. I am very sorry if this is the case. All I ask is that you read it in full before making any decisions or judgements.

I was a very young officer in the British Army during the Troubles in 1982. You will no doubt recognise my name and know that I was implicated in the tragic death of your younger brother Gerald and as you will remember, I was put on trial and subsequently cleared.

I have always felt a huge sense of shame and guilt about your brother's untimely death at sixteen years of age. I also am aware that you and your family will feel hatred towards me and the British Army, and that is perfectly understandable, given the circumstances at the time.

I now live in the Greek Islands and have been recently diagnosed with untreatable cancer. I'm attempting to put my affairs in order and I want to make some sort of reparation and apology for my past and to those I have hurt. I am asking you, Father, if you would consider my offer to meet me and listen to what I have to say.

I appreciate that it is asking a lot of you - to come all the way out to Greece and the finance and inconvenience that will entail. I would not blame you if you told me to go to hell. My address and phone numbers are noted below."

Yours Sincerely

Donald Ruthven OBE: Major Ret'd

'Fucking hell! Oh.. sorry,' Simon exclaimed.

Seamus held his hand up. 'It's fine. I'm a priest not a prude.'

Simon handed the email back to Seamus. He drank some of his beer and set his glass down. 'I've known Ruthven for years. We've never got on. This is getting weirder and weirder - you're not going to believe this... but he's also contacted *me*, to say much the same thing - he's found religion and wants to make things right - for the dreadful way he's treated Siobhan and me over the years. I've only just heard about this myself today - from my friend Jude - she's friends with Ruthven's wife. I had a massive bust up with him last year - not that long after Siobhan died. It was pretty nasty actually. He spoke about her as if she was a piece of shit - so I decked him. He tried to get me charged for assault. Luckily his wife persuaded him to drop the charges. That's why I'm very cynical about all this.'

'I can't believe what I'm hearing, Si. I'm sorry about your wife by the way - Siobhan. How awful for you.'

'Thanks, it was very sudden.

'Going back to the new-found religion thing. Sometimes, in my experience - when people are facing death they can do some pretty strange things,' Seamus said, reaching for another cigarette. 'What are you going to do about him asking to meet you?

'I told Jude that it's not going to happen - ever... You're in a different circumstance Seamus - you need to make your own mind up.' Simon replied.

'Of course - of course. I've come a long way... and I need some answers.'

***

The next few days went smoothly, the guests became browner and more relaxed around one another and dropped their everyday masks. Simon told Aisha she'd found a rhythm to her teaching and he noticed that she was learning to pace herself in the heat and cope with the exertion of teaching fifteen people and all the other things that were needed to run a successful new retreat. Simon was doing more than his fair share and even found time to run a short, impromptu creative writing workshop. It was surprisingly well attended and he discovered he had a skill for inspiring and motivating the writers. Some of them produced stunning work and most hadn't done anything like this since their school days.

He said to Aisha that most couples would have struggled working in such close proximity, especially on a new venture - but they were learning how to skilfully navigate potentially stormy seas and knew when to give the other some breathing space. He felt that he fell into his natural role of night owl running the bar and the banter with the guests and Aisha was more of a lark, up at birdsong, full of energy for the day ahead. Things were looking good.

26
A SUCCESSFUL WEEK

Simon had spoken to Aisha about the developments with Ruthven and they had agreed that, even though Simon didn't want to see him, or hear his apologies - that he would accompany his old friend - to provide moral support.

The last night party had a wonderful energy. All the guests had bonded, some more intimately than others. Dimitroula, Maria and Katerina had set up a sumptuous buffet, full of Greek delights, such as Kleftiko, Souvlaki, Moussaka and several salads and vegetable dishes.

There was a buzz in the air and people sat eating and drinking and dancing on the patio area near the bar. They were talking animatedly about their wonderful week. Some of them were having a bit of a sing song - and a couple of romances had flourished under the Greek sun. Aisha brought out some guitars, maracas and african drums for people to use - and there were some amazingly talented musicians and singers. She had already held her final closing session with the guests. It turned out to be quite emotional for everyone - as she'd grown close to her little group over the course of the week.

Carla, a young blond Swedish woman walked over somewhat unsteadily to the centre of the throng, and tapped a spoon on her wine glass. After a few false starts the noise quietened down a bit, enabling her to be heard.

'Ladies and gentlemen. Can I just say a big thank you to all the staff here for a wonderful and inspiring week - especially Aisha... and her lovely partner Simon... Dimitroula and Maria and Katerina too - thanks so much for looking after us this week ... and not forgetting Olive the Retreat cat.' A cheer went up. 'I know that none of us wants to leave this beautiful paradise - but I for one will be coming back next year.' Cue for more loud cheering and whooping.

Simon and Aisha walked hand in hand over to the guests and beckoned Dimitroula and Maria and Katerina over. Simon motioned for Aisha to take centre stage. It took a little while for the noise to die down.

'Thank you so much everyone, we couldn't have done it without you all and we couldn't have done it without the superb culinary skills of Dimitroula and her helpers Maria and Katerina. Please take a bow ladies.'

The three women gave a little wave and their faces were wreathed in smiles. 'Thanks to Simon for running the bar this week, although... I think he's drunk all the profits himself.' Laughter rang out and Simon held his hand up.

'Guilty as charged,' he smiled.

The celebrations carried on long into the hot night and one by one the guests drifted reluctantly back to their rooms. Soon there was only Aisha, Simon and Seamus left at the bar.

'I can't thank you both enough for agreeing that Si comes with me next week. I know that you wanted to avoid seeing Ruthven and how difficult it's going to be for you Si. I'm not looking forward to it either - but like I said, I need answers. I may not get them of course. I can't be a hypocrite about this either. I did my fair share of violence too - as I said Si, being a priest doesn't make you a saint or a better person than everyone else. I regret so many of the things I did.'

Aisha put her hand on Seamus's shoulder.

'We are all human. We all make mistakes and we all have regrets. I hope you get those answers and that the visit gives you some sort of peace of mind.'

'Thank you my dear. Those are wise words. Si told me about your past in Sarajevo - so I know you've lived through a lot too.'

Aisha smiled. 'Thank you. These things were tough at the time - but they make us the people we are today.'

Breakfast on the last day was subdued, some guests were nursing hangovers and some were simply sad at having to leave. Simon and Aisha were bustling about, organising people's luggage and ensuring Michaelis and his minibus came in plenty of time.

There were some tears and lots of farewell hugs as the guests boarded the little bus. Many of them promised to come back next year. There was an eerie silence as the bus drove out of sight and Simon and Aisha stopped waving. Dimitroula and Maria and Katerina joined them for a well earned coffee and informal debrief of the week. Everyone agreed that it had been a huge success. A few tweaks were needed here and there but it had been a fantastic, if tiring week. The cleaners had started arriving to get the place ready for the next course in a week's time. Everyone was secretly glad to be having a bit of a breather before the sea kayaking week. Simon and Aisha were expecting a bit of an easier time compared to the last hectic week. The cooks would prepare a picnic lunch every day, as the guests would be out all day. Simon would of course still run the bar.

***

They had moved back to their house. Both of them had a well earned long lie on Sunday morning and they were looking forward to having a leisurely lunch at the taverna with Seamus and a few days off before the Sea Kayaking week. It seemed ages since they'd seen Panos and Eleni, although they weren't sure how much time they'd have to chat to them. The tourist season was now in full swing and the weather was scorching, now that it was mid - June. They were a bit late arriving at the taverna and it was busy. Panos was carrying trays of food and he waved as they came in and beckoned them over. Simon noted that Roula and Dimitri were helping out and Eleni was dashing about with trays of food and drink.

'Good afternoon my friends.' Panos came over and hugged them both. Eleni waved briefly and scuttled back into the kitchen.

'We're having a busy one.'

'So I see,' Simon replied.

Panos lowered his voice and leaned closer. 'In case I don't get another chance, I just want to wish you luck when you see Mr Ruthven next week. I admire you for helping out your friend.'

'Thanks mate. I'm dreading it actually.'

'You will be fine and then you can get on with your life. Seamus is already here by the way. He's just having a drink and some snacks while he waits. He seems like a lovely gentleman, or should I say... a lovely priest. We had a very brief chat. I'll get you some drinks,' Panos said and handed them a menu each. 'New menu for the new season,' he smiled, and went back to the counter for more orders.

Panos had reserved their favourite table near the bar. Seamus greeted his friends.

'I see you've made yourself at home there mate,' Simon said.

'I got here a wee bit early, it's Sunday after all, and I'm used to waking early - as you can imagine. Panos and Eleni have been looking after me,' Seamus smiled broadly and took a large swig of his beer.

Of course - years of Sunday routine eh?' Simon said.

Panos brought the drinks over and sat down beside them with a small glass of Mythos. 'I have a two minute break,' he smiled. 'It's great to see you two. It feels like ages and it's lovely to meet you, Seamus.

'And for me to meet you and your lovely family Panos. Simon and Aisha have told me lots about you and how you're such great friends.'

'We go back many years - just like you two. I am so glad the first week went well for them.'

Did you make much profit from the bar mate?' Panos asked.

'Aisha said I drank most of the profits.' Simon put his hand on her arm and smiled.

'No surprise to me,' Panos winked at Aisha.

'I think I helped with the profits too, Panos, a lot of late nights,' Seamus said.

'I think you may have helped just a little, Seamus,' Aisha smiled.

Eleni came bustling out of the kitchen and Aisha and Simon took turns to give her a huge hug.

'It's great to see you both. It seems like such a long time,' Eleni said.

'Panos said the same,' Aisha replied.

'And I hear that your first ever week was a huge success. Congratulations. You must be so pleased.'

'Thanks so much. It was even better than we'd ever dreamt it would be,' Aisha replied.

'We'll celebrate with you when it quietens down after lunch. It's a bit mad today.' Eleni said.

'Good for profits though,' Panos said, smiling and rubbing the fingers of his right hand together and smiling like a Corfu cat.

27
SHOWDOWN

The car came to a halt outside Major and Mrs Ruthven's house and the wheels made a crunching sound on the gravel.

Simon took hold of Seamus's arm. 'I just want to say something before we go in mate...I don't want to be melodramatic - but we could be walking into a trap here. I'm still very cynical about his motives. You don't know him like I do - he's a nasty piece of work.'

'Understood Si. Don't forget I hate him too - and I've never even met him. Let's just keep our wits about us.'

Simon nodded. 'Ok let's get this over with.'

Both men got out of the car and into the midday sunshine and began walking towards the front door. Simon rang the doorbell twice and the familiar tune of *Land of Hope and Glory rang out*. He and Seamus looked at one another and suppressed the urge to laugh and it helped to dissolve the tension - temporarily at least.

After what seemed an eternity, the door slowly opened and a tall, thin, grey haired lady, wearing a blue Summer dress, stood facing them.

'Good morning gentlemen.' She smiled and glanced down at her watch. 'Or should I say good afternoon,' she said in cut glass tones.

'Good afternoon Mrs Ruthven, this is my friend Father Seamus Kelly.'

'Jude explained the incredible set of circumstances that brought you both here. And that you're friends from many years ago in Belfast. Life can be very strange indeed,' Jenny said.

it's lovely to meet you Ma'am,' Seamus said, gently shaking her hand. 'Under the circumstances.'

'Oh call me Jenny, makes me feel like an old woman otherwise, which of course I am. But please indulge me...just for today.' she smiled. 'Come through. Don's with his carers at the moment, they're making him presentable.'

The men exchanged nervous smiles as they followed Jenny into the lounge area, which had a huge bay window. Jude got up from the couch and she walked over to greet them. She gave them both a hug. 'Lovely to meet you Seamus, or should I say Father Seamus.'

He smiled and touched her arm. 'Seamus will do just fine Jude. I'm on holiday my dear.'

Jenny went over to a large table where pots of tea and coffee and a mound of small, exquisitely cut sandwiches and cakes and biscuits had been set out. Years of being an army wife had conditioned Jenny to be a most organised and considerate host. From the black tie colonial dinner parties in exotic Singapore to the mundane coffee mornings on drab army housing estates of Aldershot. Jenny had learned the art of small talk and how to look after people and put them at ease.

'Please sit down gentlemen and make yourselves comfortable. Now, would you like tea or coffee...or something stronger?'

'Tea's fine for me Jenny,' Seamus said.

'Coffee Jenny, two sugars please,' Simon replied, resisting the strong urge to ask for a dutch courage whisky.

Both men sat down and had a look around the room. There were several photos of the Major in uniform and plenty with him and his wife, including a black and white one of their wedding day. There were some other photos of a young couple with children, presumably their children and grandchildren and his other military momentos were sprinkled about the place.

'How was the drive over darling?' Jude asked, making small talk.

'It was fine Jude, it's a while since I've been this far east of the island,' Simon said. He felt his stomach churning with nerves.

'You have a grand view here Jenny - it's stunning,' Seamus said admiringly.

Jenny brought over two plates of sandwiches. 'Thank you, yes we're very lucky to live here. It feels a bit remote at times, but at least we don't get many tourists bothering us.'

Everyone burst out into nervous laughter and Jenny's hand flew to her mouth and her face flushed pink.

'Oh my goodness, I'm so sorry, I didn't mean to be rude. I know that you're here on holiday Seamus, please excuse my manners.'

Seamus smiled. 'It's fine Jenny, I wouldn't want tourists bothering me either if I lived in such a peaceful place. No offence taken my dear.' He bit into a tiny cucumber sandwich,'

'It's usually me who puts their damn foot in it isn't it Jenny!' The major's deep booming tones cut the quiet atmosphere like a knife, startling everyone. Major Ruthven was being pushed into the room in a wheelchair by one of his carers.

Jenny put her hand on her chest. 'Don, you gave us all a fright there. You should have warned me.' She got up from her chair and took the wheelchair from his carer, and smoothed his hair. Simon noticed a small oxygen tank at the side of the wheelchair with a mask attached.

'Thank you Athena. I'll take over, go and have your break sweetie, you've been up since the crack of dawn, you must be tired and hungry.'

'Efharisto Madam,' Athena replied, as she left the room.

Simon noted Donald Ruthven's breathing was wheezing and laboured. He had a blue woollen blanket around his shoulders and another one over his knees. Simon thought that he'd aged considerably since he'd seen him less than a year ago.

'Don, this is Father Seamus Kelly,' Jenny explained. 'You know Simon of course.'

Donald nodded. Simon gave him a brief glance. He was finding it hard to mask the loathing he was feeling towards him.

Seamus had waited nearly forty years for this moment and now he was feet away from the man who had killed his sixteen year old brother. 'Thank you for inviting me Major,' he said, in a strained voice.

Jenny continued. 'Don's asked me to say a few words before *he* speaks. He has to limit how much he talks...He was diagnosed with untreatable lung cancer six months ago. It was a shock to us and our son and daughter - we have grandchildren too. He's never been a particularly religious man, but a few months ago he received a visit from Father James, the local Anglican priest...there's a small church on the island. Father James is a lovely man, and so patient. Don didn't make him feel welcome at first but they gradually hit it off. He got him thinking about things from his past and his Army days. Over to you Don.

'Thank you Jenny. I know that today...is not easy for any of us,' he said slowly and with some difficulty...'so...I won't waste words. Firstly... Mr McCardle, I should say, Simon...I am sincerely and genuinely sorry - for the way I've treated you and your late wife over the years. I've been boorish and insensitive - not to say cruel. I should not have allowed my own personal prejudices to influence my behaviour. And that includes the disgusting things I said at Jude's party last year.'

Simon took an age to respond. 'Grudgingly accepted. I'm not buying this religious conversion by the way. I'm sorry Jenny - but too much has happened. I'm only here to give Seamus some moral support.'

Jenny nodded and gave a thin smile.

Donald nodded and continued. 'Father Kelly. I want to thank you for travelling all the way out here. That can't have been an easy thing to do....As I said in my email... I was charged with the murder of your younger brother Gerald, for a tragic incident that happened during a riot in Belfast in 1982. I was a raw young officer then, wet behind the ears and was only a few weeks into my regiment's tour of duty.' He paused to gather his breath... 'I was tried in court, as you know. The circumstances are well recorded, but I want to give you *my* version...I hadn't been in the army very long, when I got posted to Belfast. I never meant to shoot at, never mind kill your brother, despite what some people said.... I have no reason to lie - especially now? I can, however, totally understand why they thought I deliberately killed Gerald. Feelings were running very high in Belfast at that time. It was a tinderbox - waiting to ignite.'

Seamus was listening intently.

'It was bloody chaos that night. There were petrol bombs and bricks coming at us from all angles...then we heard gunfire and two soldiers in my section were shot, one fatally. Things escalated very quickly. We were terrified. This was a different ball game now. I noticed a man pointing a rifle at us, from a shop doorway. I aimed at him and fired. At the last minute someone ran in front of him. I didn't even see him, he was just a blur. As you now know...it was your brother Gerald. I shot him by mistake. And please God...believe me, it was....a tragic mistake.

Seamus stared straight ahead, his face a mask of barely concealed hatred.

'I am *so* sorry Father Seamus. If I could turn the clock back I would... I know you won't believe me, but hardly a day goes by that I don't think about it.'

The silence was deafening. Seamus took some time to reply.

'How do you think me and my family felt when this happened Major? ...You probably got a nice shiny medal for your service. And what did my family get? A few pounds...in what they laughingly called *compensation* - from the British government. Mammie died at forty eight - of a broken heart. My Da drank himself to death.

Jenny dabbed her eyes with a tissue.

Seamus continued. 'Why should I believe you? I've been carrying this for nearly forty years...since I was eighteen. I've fantasised about meeting you and...yes killing you ... with my bare hands...wearing a dog collar doesn't make you a saint - nor does it make you immune to hatred and anger.

'And yes - I did things that caused people to be hurt. So... who am I to judge you might ask? It seems crazy now, we were all young men, about the same age as your squaddies. We should have been going to the pub, or a football game together - but we spent our time - trying to kill each other - madness, utter madness...but you had your job to do, and we had ours.'

Seamus gazed out at the sea in the far distance. Simon thought that his friend was now somewhere else... forty years ago - in the back streets of Belfast.

Seamus drank his cold tea and continued. 'Gerry was a great footballer - he had a trial for Man United lined up. I was jealous of him, *I* wanted to be the next George Best, we all did. But Gerry *could* have been - they reckoned he was that good. I can still see him now...kicking a dirty old plastic ball about our street...we couldn't afford a proper one. I remember it like it was yesterday....I remember his smile...he had a lovely wee smile.'

Donald Ruthven wiped his eyes with the back of his hand. Jenny passed him a tissue. His voice sounded tortured... I'm not asking you to forgive me Father. I can't expect that, but I was a frightened twenty three year old. I was a trained soldier though and I should have checked again before firing - but... I panicked. I was terrified and I thought I was going to die.'

Seamus sat like a statue for at least a minute and then took a tissue out of his pocket and dabbed his eyes. He stood up and slowly walked over towards Donald Ruthven and very carefully and deliberately offered his hand. Donald looked unsure, then he pushed out his large bony hand.

'If it's important to you - I forgive you...I forgive you - because I want to believe that you're telling the truth, but who's going to forgive *me* Donald?'

'I can't answer that, but I sincerely hope you find it. Thank you Father Seamus. You're a good man, and you're in the right job,' Donald replied.

Seamus responded. 'I remember the old American presenter Walter Cronkite saying...'*War of course is a form of madness. It's hardly a civilised pursuit. It's amazing how we spend so much time inventing devices to kill each other and so little time working on how to achieve peace."*

Donald nodded in agreement.

'Don's going to rest now. He gets so tired,' Jenny said, wearily. 'Thank you all for coming,'

'Thanks for the tea and lovely food my dear,' Seamus said, as they began to walk towards the door.

'It was my pleasure,' Jenny replied.

'And it was nice to meet you too Jude. Jenny's going to need good friends like you.'

'Thank you Father,' Jude replied. 'Bye Simon.'

'Bye Jude. We'll catch up soon. Take care Jenny,' Simon said.

Simon and Seamus got into the car and headed back on the coast road to Neo Horio in the fierce afternoon sun.

Seamus sighed. 'I don't know about you Si...but I could do with a large one."

Seamus had politely declined the offer of dinner at Simon and Aishas. He said that he'd felt completely drained and so had Simon. They met him the next morning at the port terminal, where he was catching the ferry to Crete, before flying home.

'Will you come back next year Seamus?' Aisha asked. 'We have another Yoga week in June.'

'Just try and stop me my dear,' Seamus said. 'If I don't - I'll have a face as long as a Lurgan spade. Simon will translate that later no doubt.'

Simon smiled.

'God bless you both - and good luck with the Olive Grove. You have a little gem on your hands there...and mind and look after yer man here - he always was the most sensible of all of us.'

Printed in Great Britain
by Amazon